THE SECRET PLACES
OF THE HEART

¶ Mr. WELLS has also written the following novels:

LOVE AND MR. LEWISHAM
KIPPS
MR. POLLY
THE WHEELS OF CHANCE
THE NEW MACHIAVELLI
ANN VERONICA
TONO BUNGAY
MARRIAGE
BEALBY
THE PASSIONATE FRIENDS
THE WIFE OF SIR ISAAC HAR-
MAN
THE RESEARCH MAGNIFICENT
MR. BRITLING SEES IT THROUGH
THE SOUL OF A BISHOP
JOAN AND PETER
THE UNDYING FIRE

¶ The following fantastic and imaginative romances:

THE WAR OF THE WORLDS
THE TIME MACHINE
THE WONDERFUL VISIT
THE ISLAND OF DR. MOREAU
THE SEA LADY
THE SLEEPER AWAKES
THE FOOD OF THE GODS
THE WAR IN THE AIR
THE FIRST MEN IN THE MOON
IN THE DAYS OF THE COMET
THE WORLD SET FREE

And numerous Short Stories now collected in One Volume under the title of

THE COUNTRY OF THE BLIND

¶ A Series of books upon Social, Religious, and Political questions:

ANTICIPATIONS (1900)
MANKIND IN THE MAKING
FIRST AND LAST THINGS
NEW WORLDS FOR OLD
A MODERN UTOPIA
THE FUTURE IN AMERICA
AN ENGLISHMAN LOOKS AT THE
WORLD
WHAT IS COMING?
WAR AND THE FUTURE
IN THE FOURTH YEAR
GOD THE INVISIBLE KING
THE OUTLINE OF HISTORY
RUSSIA IN THE SHADOWS
THE SALVAGING OF CIVILIZA-
TION
WASHINGTON AND THE HOPE OF
PEACE

¶ And two little books about children's play, called:

FLOOR GAMES and LITTLE WARS

THE SECRET PLACES OF THE HEART

BY

H. G. WELLS

New York
THE MACMILLAN COMPANY
1922

CONTENTS

THE SECRET PLACES
OF THE HEART

CHAPTER THE FIRST

THE CONSULTATION

§ 1

THE maid was a young woman of great natural calmness; she was accustomed to let in visitors who had this air of being annoyed and finding one umbrella too numerous for them. It mattered nothing to her that the gentleman was asking for Dr. Martineau as if he was asking for something with an unpleasant taste. Almost imperceptibly she relieved him of his umbrella and juggled his hat and coat on to a massive mahogany stand. "What name, Sir?" she asked, holding open the door of the consulting room.

"Hardy," said the gentleman, and then yielding it reluctantly with its distasteful three-year-old honour, "Sir Richmond Hardy."

The door closed softly behind him and he found himself in undivided possession of the large indif-

1

ferent apartment in which the nervous and mental
troubles of the outer world eddied for a time on
their way to the distinguished specialist. A bowl
of daffodils, a handsome bookcase containing
bound Victorian magazines and antiquated medi-
cal works, some paintings of Scotch scenery, three
big armchairs, a buhl clock, and a bronze Dancing
Faun, by their want of any collective idea enhanced rather than mitigated the promiscuous disregard of the room. He drifted to the midmost
of the three windows and stared out despondently
at Harley Street.

For a minute or so he remained as still and limp
as an empty jacket on its peg, and then a gust of
irritation stirred him.

"Damned fool I was to come here," he said.
. . . "*Damned* fool!

"Rush out of the place? . . .

"I've given my name." . . .

He heard the door behind him open and for a
moment pretended not to hear. Then he turned
round. "I don't see what you can do for me,"
he said.

"I'm sure *I* don't," said the doctor. "People
come here and talk."

There was something reassuringly inaggressive
about the figure that confronted Sir Richmond.
Dr. Martineau's height wanted at least three
inches of Sir Richmond's five feet eleven; he was
humanly plump, his face was round and pink and

cheerfully wistful, a little suggestive of the full moon, of what the full moon might be if it could get fresh air and exercise. Either his tailor had made his trousers too short or he had braced them too high so that he seemed to have grown out of them quite recently. Sir Richmond had been dreading an encounter with some dominating and mesmeric personality; this amiable presence dispelled his preconceived resistances.

Dr. Martineau, a little out of breath as though he had been running upstairs, with his hands in his trouser pockets, seemed intent only on disavowals. "People come here and talk. It does them good, and sometimes I am able to offer a suggestion.

"Talking to someone who understands a little," he expanded the idea.

"I'm jangling damnably . . . overwork. . . ."

"Not overwork," Dr. Martineau corrected. "Not overwork. Overwork never hurt anyone. Fatigue stops that. A man can work—good straightforward work, without internal resistance, until he drops,—and never hurt himself. You must be working against friction."

"Friction! I'm like a machine without oil. I'm grinding to death. . . . And it's so *damned* important I *shouldn't* break down. It's *vitally* important."

He stressed his words and reinforced them with a quivering gesture of his upraised clenched hand. "My temper's in rags. I explode at any little thing. I'm *raw*. I can't work steadily for ten minutes and I can't leave off working."

"Your name," said the doctor, "is familiar. Sir Richmond Hardy? In the papers. What is it?"

"Fuel."

"Of course! The Fuel Commission. Stupid of me! We certainly can't afford to have you ill."

"I *am* ill. But you can't afford to have me absent from that Commission."

"Your technical knowledge——"

"Technical knowledge be damned! Those men mean to corner the national fuel supply. And waste it! For their profits. That's what I'm up against. You don't know the job I have to do. You don't know what a Commission of that sort is. The moral tangle of it. You don't know how its possibilities and limitations are canvassed and schemed about, long before a single member is appointed. Old Cassidy worked the whole thing with the prime minister. I can see that now as plain as daylight. I might have seen it at first. . . . Three experts who'd been got at; they thought *I*'d been got at; two Labour men who'd do anything you wanted them to do provided you called them 'level-headed.' Wagstaffe the socialist art critic who could be trusted to play the fool and make nationalization look silly, and the rest mine owners, railway managers, oil profiteers, financial adventurers. . . ."

He was fairly launched. "It's the blind folly
of it! In the days before the war it was different.
Then there was abundance. A little grabbing or
cornering was all to the good. All to the good.
It prevented things being used up too fast. And
the world was running by habit; the inertia was
tremendous. You could take all sorts of liberties.
But all this is altered. We're living in a different
world. The public won't stand things it used to
stand. It's a new public. It's—wild. It'll smash
up the show if they go too far. Everything short
and running shorter—food, fuel, material. But
these people go on. They go on as though nothing had changed. . . . Strikes, Russia, nothing
will warn them. There are men on that Commission who would steal the brakes off a mountain
railway just before they went down in it. . . . It's
a struggle with suicidal imbeciles. It's——! But
I'm talking! I didn't come here to talk Fuel."

"You think there may be a smash-up?"

"I lie awake at night, thinking of it."

"A social smash-up."

"Economic. Social. Yes. Don't you?"

"A social smash-up seems to me altogether a
possibility. All sorts of people I find think that,"
said the doctor. "All sorts of people lie awake
thinking of it."

"I wish some of my damned Committee would!"

The doctor turned his eyes to the window. "I lie
awake too," he said and seemed to reflect. But he

was observing his patient acutely—with his ears.

"But you see how important it is," said Sir Richmond, and left his sentence unfinished.

"I'll do what I can for you," said the doctor, and considered swiftly what line of talk he had best follow.

§ 2

"This sense of a coming smash is epidemic," said the doctor. "It's at the back of all sorts of mental trouble. It is a new state of mind. Before the war it was abnormal—a phase of neurasthenia. Now it is almost the normal state with whole classes of intelligent people. Intelligent, I say. The others always have been casual and adventurous and always will be. A loss of confidence in the general background of life. So that we seem to float over abysses."

"We do," said Sir Richmond.

"And we have nothing but the old habits and ideas acquired in the days of our assurance. There is a discord, a jarring."

The doctor pursued his train of thought. "A new, raw and dreadful sense of responsibility for the universe. Accompanied by a realization that the job is overwhelmingly too big for us."

"We've got to stand up to the job," said Sir Richmond. "Anyhow, what else is there to do?

We *may* keep things together. . . . I've got to do my bit. And if only I could hold myself at it, I could beat those fellows. But that's where the devil of it comes in. Never have I been so desirous to work well in my life. And never have I been so slack and weak-willed and inaccurate. . . . Sloppy. . . . Indolent. . . . *Vicious!* . . ."

The doctor was about to speak, but Sir Richmond interrupted him. "What's got hold of me? What's got hold of me? I used to work well enough. It's as if my will had come untwisted and was ravelling out into separate strands. I've lost my unity. I'm not a man but a mob. I've got to recover my vigour. At any cost."

Again as the doctor was about to speak the word was taken out of his mouth. "And what I think of it, Dr. Martineau, is this: it's fatigue. It's mental and moral fatigue. Too much effort. On too high a level. And too—austere. One strains and fags. *Flags!* 'Flags' I meant to say. One strains and flags and then the lower stuff in one, the subconscious stuff, takes control."

There was a flavour of popularized psychoanalysis about this, and the doctor drew in the corners of his mouth and gave his head a critical slant. "M'm." But this only made Sir Richmond raise his voice and quicken his speech. "I want," he said, "a good tonic. A pick-me-up, a stimulating harmless drug of some sort. That's indicated anyhow. To begin with. Something to pull me together, as people say. Bring me up to the scratch again.''

''I don't like the use of drugs,'' said the doctor.

The expectation of Sir Richmond's expression changed to disappointment. ''But that's not reasonable,'' he cried. ''That's not reasonable. That's superstition. Call a thing a drug and condemn it! Everything is a drug. Everything that affects you. Food stimulates or tranquillizes. Drink. Noise is a stimulant and quiet an opiate. What is life but response to stimulants? Or reaction after them? When I'm exhausted I want food. When I'm overactive and sleepless I want tranquillizing. When I'm dispersed I want pulling together.''

''But we don't know how to use drugs,'' the doctor objected.

''But you ought to know.''

Dr. Martineau fixed his eye on a first floor window sill on the opposite side of Harley Street. His manner suggested a lecturer holding on to his theme.

''A day will come when we shall be able to manipulate drugs—all sorts of drugs—and work them in to our general way of living. I have no prejudice against them at all. A time will come when we shall correct our moods, get down to our reserves of energy by their help, suspend fatigue, put off sleep during long spells of exertion. At some sudden crisis for example. When we shall know enough to know just how far to go with this, that or the other stuff. And how to wash out its after effects. . . . I quite agree with you,—in principle. . . . But that time hasn't come yet. . . . Decades of research yet. . . . If we tried that sort of thing now, we should be like children playing with poisons and explosives. . . . It's out of the question.''

''I've been taking a few little things already. Easton Syrup for example.''

''Strychnine. It carries you for a time and drops you by the way. Has it done you any good —any *nett* good? It has—I can see—broken your sleep.''

The doctor turned round again to his patient and looked up into his troubled face.

''Given physiological trouble I don't mind resorting to a drug. Given structural injury I don't mind surgery. But except for any little mischief your amateur drugging may have done you do not seem to me to be either sick or injured. You've no trouble either of structure or material. You're —worried—ill in your mind, and otherwise perfectly sound. It's the current of your thoughts, fermenting. If the trouble is in the mental sphere, why go out of the mental sphere for a treatment? Talk and thought; these are your remedies. Cool deliberate thought. You're unravelled. You say it yourself. Drugs will only make this or that unravelled strand behave disproportionately. You don't want that. You want to take stock of yourself as a whole—find out where you stand.''

''But the Fuel Commission?''

''Is it sitting now?''

''Adjourned till after Whitsuntide. But there's heaps of work to be done.

''Still,'' he added, ''this is my one chance of any treatment.''

The doctor made a little calculation. ''Three weeks. . . . It's scarcely time enough to begin.''

''You're certain that no regimen of carefully planned and chosen tonics——''

''Dismiss the idea. Dismiss it.'' He decided to take a plunge. ''I've just been thinking of a little holiday for myself. But I'd like to see you through this. And if I am to see you through, there ought to be some sort of beginning now. In this three weeks. Suppose. . . .''

Sir Richmond leapt to his thought. ''I'm free to go anywhere.''

''Golf would drive a man of your composition mad?''

''It would.''

''That's that. Still—. . . The country must be getting beautiful again now,—after all the rain we have had. I have a little two-seater. I don't know. . . . The repair people promise to release it before Friday.''

"But *I* have a choice of two very comfortable little cars. Why not be my guest?"

"That might be more convenient."

"I'd prefer my own car."

"Then what do you say?"

"I agree. Peripatetic treatment."

"South and west. We could talk on the road. In the evenings. By the wayside. We might make the beginnings of a treatment. . . . A simple tour. Nothing elaborate. You wouldn't bring a man?"

"I always drive myself."

§ 3

"There's something very pleasant," said the doctor, envisaging his own rash proposal, "in travelling along roads you don't know and seeing houses and parks and villages and towns for which you do not feel in the slightest degree responsible. They hide all their troubles from the road. Their backyards are tucked away out of sight, they show a brave face; there's none of the nasty self-betrayals of the railway approach. And everything will be fresh still. There will still be a lot of apple-blossom—and bluebells. . . . And all the while we can be getting on with your affair."

He was back at the window now. "I want the holiday myself," he said.

He addressed Sir Richmond over his shoulder. "Have you noted how fagged and unstable *everybody* is getting? Everybody intelligent, I mean."

"It's an infernally worrying time."

"Exactly. Everybody suffers."

"It's no *good* going on in the old ways——"

"It isn't. And it's a frightful strain to get into any new ways. So here we are.

"A man," the doctor expanded, "isn't a creature in vacuo. He's himself and his world. He's a surface of contact, a system of adaptations, between his essential self and his surroundings. Well, our surroundings have become—how shall I put it?—a landslide. The war which seemed such a definable catastrophe in 1914 was, after all, only the first loud crack and smash of the collapse. The war is over and—nothing is over. This peace is a farce, reconstruction an exploded phrase. The slide goes on,—it goes, if anything, faster, without a sign of stopping. And all our poor little adaptations! Which we have been elaborating and trusting all our lives! . . . One after another they fail us. We are stripped. . . . We have to begin all over again. . . . I'm fifty-seven and I feel at times nowadays like a chicken new hatched in a thunderstorm."

The doctor walked towards the bookcase and turned.

"Everybody is like that. . . . It isn't—what
are you going to do? It isn't—what am I going
to do? It's—what are we all going to do? . . .
Lord! How safe and established everything was
in 1910, say. We talked of this great war that was
coming, but nobody thought it would come. We
had been born in peace, comparatively speaking;
we had been brought up in peace. There was talk
of wars. There were wars—little wars—that altered nothing material. . . . Consols used to be
at 112 and you fed your household on ten shillings
a head a week. You could run over all Europe,
barring Turkey and Russia, without even a pass-
port. You could get to Italy in a day. Never
were life and comfort so safe—for respectable
people. And we *were* respectable people. . . .
That was the world that made us what we are.
That was the sheltering and friendly greenhouse
in which we grew. We fitted our minds to that.
. . . And here we are with the greenhouse falling in upon us lump by lump, smash and clatter,
the wild winds of heaven tearing in through the
gaps."

Upstairs on Dr. Martineau's desk lay the
typescript of the opening chapters of a book that
was intended to make a great splash in the world,
his *Psychology of a New Age*. He had his meta-
phors ready.

"We said: 'This system will always go on. We
needn't bother about it.' We just planned our

lives accordingly. It was like a bird building its nest of frozen snakes. My father left me a decent independence. I developed my position; I have lived between here and the hospital, doing good work, enormously interested, prosperous, mildly distinguished. I had been born and brought up on the good ship Civilization. I assumed that some-one else was steering the ship all right. I never knew; I never enquired.''

"Nor did I,'' said Sir Richmond, "but——''

"And nobody was steering the ship,'' the doctor went on. "Nobody had ever steered the ship. It was adrift.''

"I realized that. I——''

"It is a new realization. Always hitherto men have lived by faith—as children do, as the animals do. At the back of the healthy mind, human or animal, has been this persuasion: 'This is all right. This will go on. If I keep the rule, if I do so and so, all will be well. I need not trouble further; things are cared for.' ''

"If we could go on like that!'' said Sir Richmond.

"We can't. That faith is dead. The war—and the peace—have killed it.''

The doctor's round face became speculative. His resemblance to the full moon increased. He seemed to gaze at remote things. "It may very well be that man is no more capable of living out of that atmosphere of assurance than a tadpole is

of living out of water. His mental existence may
be conditional on that. Deprived of it he may become incapable of sustained social life. He may
become frantically self-seeking—incoherent . . .
a stampede. . . . Human sanity may—*disperse*.

"That's our trouble," the doctor completed.
"Our fundamental trouble. All our confidences
and our accustomed adaptations are destroyed.
We fit together no longer. We are—loose. We
don't know where we are nor what to do. The
psychology of the former time fails to give safe
responses, and the psychology of the New Age
has still to develop."

§ 4

"That is all very well," said Sir Richmond in
the resolute voice of one who will be pent no
longer. "That is all very well as far as it goes.
But it does not cover my case. I am not suffering
from inadaptation. I *have* adapted. I have
thought things out. I think—much as you do.
Much as you do. So it's not that. But—— . . .
Mind you, I am perfectly clear where I am. Where
we are. What is happening to us all is the break-
up of the entire system. Agreed! We have to
make another system or perish amidst the wreck-
age. I see that clearly. Science and plan have
to replace custom and tradition in human affairs.
Soon. Very soon. Granted. Granted. We used

to say all that. Even before the war. Now
we mean it. We've muddled about in the old
ways overlong. Some new sort of world, planned
and scientific, has to be got going. Civilization renewed. Rebuilding civilization—while the prem-
ises are still occupied and busy. It's an immense
enterprise, but it is the only thing to be done.
In some ways it's an enormously attractive enterprise. Inspiring. It grips my imagination. I
think of the other men who must be at work.
Working as I do rather in the dark as yet. With
whom I shall presently join up. . . . The attempt
may fail; all things human may fail; but on the
other hand it may succeed. I never had such
faith in anything as I have in the rightness of the
work I am doing now. I begin at that. But here
is where my difficulty comes in. The top of my
brain, my innermost self says all that I have been
saying, but—— The rest of me won't follow.
The rest of me refuses to attend, forgets, strag-
gles, misbehaves.''

''Exactly.''

The word irritated Sir Richmond. ''Not 'exactly' at all. 'Amazingly,' if you like. . . . I
have this unlimited faith in our present tremendous necessity—for work—for devotion; I believe
my share, the work I am doing, is essential to
the whole thing—and I work sluggishly. I work
reluctantly. I work damnably.''

''Exact——'' The doctor checked himself. ''All

that is explicable. Indeed it is. Listen for a moment to me! Consider what you are. Consider what we are. Consider what a man is before you marvel at his ineptitudes of will. Face the accepted facts. Here is a creature not ten thousand generations from the ape, his ancestor. Not ten thousand. And that ape again, not a score of thousands from the monkey, his forebear. A man's body, his bodily powers, are just the body and powers of an ape, a little improved, a little adapted to novel needs. That brings me to my point. *Can his mind and will be anything better?* For a few generations, a few hundreds at most, knowledge and wide thought have flared out on the darknesses of life. . . . But the substance of man is ape still. He may carry a light in his brain, but his instincts move in the darkness. Out of that darkness he draws his motives.''

''Or fails to draw them,'' said Sir Richmond.

''Or fails. . . . And that is where these new methods of treatment come in. We explore that failure. Together. What the psychoanalyst does—and I will confess that I owe much to the psychoanalyst—what he does is to direct thwarted, disappointed and perplexed people to the realities of their own nature. Which they have been accustomed to ignore and forget. They come to us with high ambitions or lovely illusions about themselves, torn, shredded, spoilt. They are morally denuded. Dreams they hate pursue them;

abhorrent desires draw them; they are the prey of irresistible yet uncongenial impulses; they succumb to black despairs. The first thing we ask them is this: 'What else could you expect?' "

"What else could I expect?" Sir Richmond repeated, looking down on him. "H'm!"

"The wonder is not that you are sluggish, reluctantly unselfish, inattentive, spasmodic. The wonder is that you are ever anything else. . . . Do you realize that a few million generations ago, everything that stirs in us, everything that exalts human life, self-devotions, heroisms, the utmost triumphs of art, the love—for love it is—that makes you and me care indeed for the fate and welfare of all this round world, was latent in the body of some little lurking beast that crawled and hid among the branches of vanished and forgotten Mesozoic trees? A petty egg-laying, bristle-covered beast it was, with no more of the rudiments of a soul than bare hunger, weak lust and fear. . . . People always seem to regard that as a curious fact of no practical importance. It isn't: it's a vital fact of the utmost practical importance. That is what you are made of. Why should you expect—because a war and a revolution have shocked you—that you should suddenly be able to reach up and touch the sky?"

"H'm!" said Sir Richmond. "Have I been touching the sky?"

"You are trying to play the part of an honest rich man."

"I don't care to see the whole system go smash."

"Exactly," said the doctor, before he could prevent himself.

"But is it any good to tell a man that the job he is attempting is above him—that he is just a hairy reptile twice removed—anl all that sort of thing?"

"Well, it saves him from hoping too much and being too greatly disappointed. It recalls him to the proportions of the job. He gets something done by not attempting everything. . . . And it clears him up. We get him to look into himself, to see directly and in measurable terms what it is that puts him wrong and holds him back. He's no longer vaguely incapacitated. He knows."

"That's diagnosis. That's not treatment."

"Treatment by diagnosis. To analyze a mental knot is to untie it."

"You propose that I shall spend my time, until the Commission meets, in thinking about myself. . . . I wanted to forget myself."

"Like a man who tries to forget that his petrol is running short and a cylinder missing fire. . . . No. Come back to the question of what you are," said the doctor. "A creature of the darkness with

new lights. Lit and half-blinded by science and
the possibilities of controlling the world that it
opens out. In that light your will is all for service;
you care more for mankind than for yourself.
You begin to understand something of the self
beyond your self. But it is a partial and a shaded
light as yet; a little area about you it makes clear,
the rest is still the old darkness—of millions of
intense and narrow animal generations. . . . You
are like someone who awakens out of an imme-
morial sleep to find himself in a vast chamber, in a
great and ancient house, a great and ancient house
high amidst frozen and lifeless mountains—in a
sunless universe. You are not alone in it. You
are not lord of all you survey. Your leadership
is disputed. The darkness even of the room you
are in is full of ancient and discarded but quite
unsubjugated powers and purposes. . . . They
thrust ambiguous limbs and claws suddenly out of
the darkness into the light of your attention. They
snatch things out of your hand, they trip your
feet and jog your elbow. They crowd and cluster
behind you. Wherever your shadow falls, they
creep right up to you, creep upon you and struggle to take possession of you. The souls of apes,
monkeys, reptiles and creeping things haunt the
passages and attics and cellars of this living
house in which your consciousness has awakened. . . ."

The doctor gave this quotation from his unpublished book the advantages of an abrupt break and a pause.

Sir Richmond shrugged his shoulders and smiled. "And you propose a vermin hunt in the old tenement?"

"The modern man has to be master in his own house. He has to take stock and know what is there."

"Three weeks of self vivisection."

"To begin with. Three weeks of perfect honesty with yourself. As an opening. . . . It will take longer than that if we are to go through with the job."

"It's a considerable—process."

"It is."

"Yet you shrink from simple things like drugs!"

"Self-knowledge—without anæsthetics."

"Has this sort of thing ever done anyone any good at all?"

"It has turned hundreds back to sanity and steady work."

"How frank are we going to be? How full are we going to be? Anyhow—we can break off at any time. . . . We'll try it. We'll try it. . . . And so for this journey into the west of England. . . . And—if we can get there—I'm not sure that we can get there—into the secret places of my heart."

CHAPTER THE SECOND

LADY HARDY

THE patient left the house with much more self-possession than he had shown when entering it. Dr. Martineau had thrust him back from his intenser prepossessions to a more generalized view of himself, had made his troubles objective and detached him from them. He could even find something amusing now in his situation. He liked the immense scope of the theoretical duet in which they had indulged. He felt that most of it was entirely true—and, in some untraceable manner, absurd. There were entertaining possibilities in the prospect of the doctor drawing him out—he himself partly assisting and partly resisting.

He was a man of extensive reservations. His private life was in some respects exceptionally private.

"I don't confide. . . . Do I even confide in myself? I imagine I do. . . . Is there anything in myself that I haven't looked squarely in the face? . . . How much are we going into? Even as regards facts?

"Does it really help a man—to see himself? . . ."

Such thoughts engaged him until he found himself in his study. His desk and his writing table were piled high with a heavy burthen of work. Still a little preoccupied with Dr. Martineau's exposition, he began to handle this confusion. . . .

At half past nine he found himself with three hours of good work behind him. It had seemed like two. He had not worked like this for many weeks. "This is very cheering," he said. "And unexpected. Can old Moon-face have hypnotized me? Anyhow— . . . Perhaps I've only imagined I was ill. . . . Dinner?" He looked at his watch and was amazed at the time. "Good Lord! I've been at it three hours. What can have happened? Funny I didn't hear the gong."

He went downstairs and found Lady Hardy reading a magazine in a dining-room armchair and finely poised between devotion and martyrdom. A shadow of vexation fell athwart his mind at the sight of her.

"I'd no idea it was so late," he said. "I heard no gong."

"After you swore so at poor Bradley I ordered that there should be no gongs when we were alone. I did come up to your door about half past eight. I crept up. But I was afraid I might upset you if I came in."

"But you've not waited——"

"I've had a mouthful of soup." Lady Hardy rang the bell.

"I've done some work at last," said Sir Richmond, astride on the hearthrug.

"I'm glad," said Lady Hardy, without gladness. "I waited for three hours."

Lady Hardy was a frail little blue-eyed woman with uneven shoulders and a delicate sweet profile. Hers was that type of face that under even the most pleasant and luxurious circumstances still looks bravely and patiently enduring. Her refinement threw a tinge of coarseness over his eager consumption of his excellent clear soup.

"What's this fish, Bradley?" he asked.

"Turbot, Sir Richmond."

"Don't you have any?" he asked his wife.

"I've had a little fish," said Lady Hardy.

When Bradley was out of the room, Sir Richmond remarked: "I saw that nerves man, Dr. Martineau, to-day. He wants me to take a holiday."

The quiet patience of the lady's manner intensified. She said nothing. A flash of resentment lit Sir Richmond's eyes. When he spoke again, he seemed to answer unspoken accusations. "Dr. Martineau's idea is that he should come with me."

The lady adjusted herself to a new point of view.

"But won't that be reminding you of your illness and worries?"

"He seems a good sort of fellow. . . . I'm inclined to like him. He'll be as good company as anyone. . . . This *tournedos* looks excellent. Have some."

"I had a little bird," said Lady Hardy, "when I found you weren't coming."

"But I say—don't wait here if you've dined. Bradley can see to me."

She smiled and shook her head with the quiet conviction of one who knew her duty better. "Perhaps I'll have a little ice pudding when it comes," she said.

Sir Richmond detested eating alone in an atmosphere of observant criticism. And he did not like talking with his mouth full to an unembarrassed interlocutor who made no conversational leads of her own. After a few mouthfuls he pushed his plate away from him. "Then let's have up the ice pudding," he said with a faint note of bitterness.

"But have you finished——?"

"The ice pudding!" he exploded wrathfully. "The ice pudding!"

Lady Hardy sat for a moment, a picture of meek distress. Then, her delicate eyebrows raised, and the corners of her mouth drooping, she touched the button of the silver table-bell.

CHAPTER THE THIRD

THE DEPARTURE

§ 1

No wise man goes out upon a novel expedition without misgivings. And between their first meeting and the appointed morning both Sir Richmond Hardy and Dr. Martineau were the prey of quite disagreeable doubts about each other, themselves, and the excursion before them. At the time of their meeting each had been convinced that he gauged the other sufficiently for the purposes of the proposed tour. Afterwards each found himself trying to recall the other with greater distinctness and able to recall nothing but queer, ominous and minatory traits. The doctor's impression of the great fuel specialist grew ever darker, leaner, taller and more impatient. Sir Richmond took on the likeness of a monster obdurate and hostile, he spread upwards until like the Djinn out of the bottle, he darkened the heavens. And he talked too much. He talked ever so much too much. . . .

Sir Richmond also thought that the doctor

talked too much. In addition, he read into his imperfect memory of the doctor's face, an expression of protruded curiosity. What was all this problem of motives and inclinations that they were "going into" so gaily? He had merely consulted the doctor on a simple, straightforward need for a nervous tonic—that was what he had needed—a tonic. Instead he had engaged himself for—he scarcely knew what—an indiscreet, indelicate, and altogether undesirable experiment in confidences.

Both men were considerably reassured when at last they set eyes on each other again. Indeed each was surprised to find something almost agreeable in the appearance of the other. Dr. Martineau at once perceived that the fierceness of Sir Richmond was nothing more than the fierceness of an overwrought man, and Sir Richmond realized at a glance that the curiosity of Dr. Martineau's bearing had in it nothing personal or base; it was just the fine alertness of the scientific mind.

Sir Richmond had arrived nearly forty minutes late, and it would have been evident to a much less highly trained observer than Dr. Martineau that some dissension had arisen between the little, lady-like, cream and black Charmeuse car and its owner. There was a faint air of resentment and protest between them. As if Sir Richmond had been in some way rude to it.

The cap of the radiator was adorned with a

little brass figure of a flying Mercury. Frozen in a sprightly attitude, its stiff bound and its fixed heavenward stare was highly suggestive of a forced and tactful disregard of current unpleasantness.

Nothing was said, however, to confirm or dispel this suspicion of a disagreement between the man and the car. Sir Richmond directed and assisted Dr. Martineau's man to adjust the luggage at the back, and Dr. Martineau watched the proceedings from his dignified front door. He was wearing a suit of fawn tweeds, a fawn Homburg hat and a light Burberry, with just that effect of special preparation for a holiday which betrays the habitually busy man. Sir Richmond's brown gauntness was, he noted, greatly set off by his suit of grey. There had certainly been some sort of quarrel. Sir Richmond was explaining the straps to Dr. Martineau's butler with the coldness a man betrays when he explains the uncongenial habits of some unloved intimate. And when the moment came to start and the little engine did not immediately respond to the electric starter, he said: "Oh! *Come* up, you——!"

His voice sank at the last word as though it was an entirely confidential communication to the little car. And it was an extremely low and disagreeable word. So Dr. Martineau decided that it was not his business to hear it. . . .

It was speedily apparent that Sir Richmond was

an experienced and excellent driver. He took the Charmeuse out into the traffic of Baker Street and westward through brisk and busy streets and roads to Brentford and Hounslow smoothly and swiftly, making a score of unhesitating and accurate decisions without apparent thought. There was very little conversation until they were through Brentford. Near Shepherd's Bush, Sir Richmond had explained, "This is not my own particular car. That was butted into at the garage this morning and its radiator cracked. So I had to fall back on this. It's quite a good little car. In its way. My wife drives it at times. It has one or two constitutional weaknesses—incidental to the make—gear-box over the back axle for example—gets all the vibration. Whole machine rather on the flimsy side. Still——"

He left the topic at that.

Dr. Martineau said something of no consequence about its being a very comfortable little car.

Somewhere between Brentford and Hounslow, Sir Richmond plunged into the matter between them. "I don't know how deep we are going into these psychological probings of yours," he said. "But I doubt very much if we shall get anything out of them."

"Probably not," said Dr. Martineau.

"After all, what I want is a tonic. I don't see that there is anything positively wrong with me. A certain lack of energy——"

"Lack of balance," corrected the doctor. "You are wasting energy upon internal friction."

"But isn't that inevitable? No machine is perfectly efficient. No man either. There is always a waste. Waste of the type; waste of the individual idiosyncrasy. This little car, for instance, isn't pulling as she ought to pull—she never does. She's low in her class. So with myself; there is a natural and necessary high rate of energy waste. Moods of apathy and indolence are natural to me. (Damn that omnibus! All over the road!)"

"We don't deny the imperfection——" began the doctor.

"One has to fit oneself to one's circumstances," said Sir Richmond, opening up another line of thought.

"We don't deny the imperfection," the doctor stuck to it. "These new methods of treatment are based on the idea of imperfection. We begin with that. I began with that last Tuesday. . . ."

Sir Richmond, too, was sticking to his argument. "A man, and for that matter the world he lives in, is a tangle of accumulations. Your psychoanalyst starts, it seems to me, with a notion of stripping down to something fundamental. The ape before us was a tangle of accumulations, just as we are. So it was with his forebears. So it has always been. All life is an endless tangle of accumulations."

"Recognize it," said the doctor.

"And then?" said Sir Richmond, controversially.

"Recognize in particular your own tangle."

"Is my particular tangle very different from the general tangle? (Oh! Damn this feeble little engine!) I am a creature of undecided will, urged on by my tangled heredity to do a score of entirely incompatible things. Mankind, all life, is that."

"But our concern is the particular score of incompatible things you are urged to do. We examine and weigh—— We weigh——"

The doctor was still saying these words when a violent and ultimately disastrous struggle began between Sir Richmond and the little Charmeuse car. The doctor stopped in mid-sentence.

It was near Taplow station that the mutual exasperation of man and machine was brought to a crisis by the clumsy emergence of a laundry cart from a side road. Sir Richmond was obliged to pull up smartly and stopped his engine. It refused an immediate obedience to the electric starter. Then it picked up, raced noisily, disengaged great volumes of bluish smoke, and displayed an unaccountable indisposition to run on any gear but the lowest. Sir Richmond thought aloud, unpleasing thoughts. He addressed the little car as a person; he referred to ancient disputes and temperamental incompatibilities. His anger betrayed him a coarse, ill-bred man. The little car quickened under his reproaches. There were some moments of hope, dashed by the necessity of going dead slow behind an interloping van. Sir Richmond did not notice the outstretched arm of the driver of the van, and stalled his engine for a second time. The electric starter refused its office altogether.

For some moments Sir Richmond sat like a man of stone.

"I must wind it up," he said at last in a profound and awful voice. "I must wind it up."

"I get out, don't I?" asked the doctor, unanswered, and did so. Sir Richmond, after a grim search and the displacement and replacement of the luggage, produced a handle from the locker at the back of the car and prepared to wind.

There was a little difficulty. "Come *up!*" he said, and the small engine roared out like a stage lion.

The two gentlemen resumed their seats. The car started and then by an unfortunate inadvertency Sir Richmond pulled the gear lever over from the first speed to the reverse. There was a metallic clangour beneath the two gentlemen, and the car slowed down and stopped although the engine was still throbbing wildly, and the dainty veil of blue smoke still streamed forward from the back of the car before a gentle breeze. The doctor got out almost precipitately, followed by a gaunt madman, mouthing vileness, who had only a minute or so before been a decent British citizen. He made scme blind lunges at the tremulous but obdurate car, but rather as if he looked for offences and accusations than for displacements to adjust. Quivering and refusing, the little car was extraordinarily like some recalcitrant little old aristocratic lady in the hands of revolutionaries, and this made the behaviour of Sir Richmond seem even more outrageous than it would otherwise have done. He stopped the engine, he went down on his hands and knees in the road to peer up at the gear-box, then without restoring the spark, he tried to wind up the engine again. He spun the little handle with an insane violence, faster and faster for—as it seemed to the doctor—the better part of a minute. Beads of perspiration appeared upon his brow and ran together; he bared his teeth in a snarl; his hat slipped over one eye. He groaned with rage. Then, using the starting handle as a club, he assailed the car. He smote the brazen Mercury from its foothold and sent it and a part of the radiator cap with it flying across the road. He beat at the wings of the bonnet, until they bent in under his blows. Finally, he hurled the starting-handle at the wind-screen and smashed it. The starting-handle rattled over the bonnet and fell to the ground. . . .

The paroxysm was over. Ten seconds later this cataclysmal lunatic had reverted to sanity—a rather sheepish sanity.

He thrust his hands into his trouser pockets

and turned his back on the car. He remarked in a voice of melancholy detachment: "It was a mistake to bring that coupé."

Dr. Martineau had assumed an attitude of trained observation on the side path. His hands rested on his hips and his hat was a little on one side. He was inclined to agree with Sir Richmond. "I don't know," he considered. "You wanted some such blow-off as this."

"Did I?"

"The energy you have! That car must be somebody's whipping boy."

"The devil it is!" said Sir Richmond, turning round sharply and staring at it as if he expected it to display some surprising and yet familiar features. Then he looked questioningly and suspiciously at his companion.

"These outbreaks do nothing to amend the originating grievance," said the doctor. "No. And at times they are even costly. But they certainly lift a burthen from the nervous system. . . . And now I suppose we have to get that little ruin to Maidenhead."

"Little ruin!" repeated Sir Richmond. "No. There's lots of life in the little beast yet."

He reflected. "She'll have to be towed." He felt in his breast pocket. "Somewhere I have the R.A.C. order paper, the Badge that will Get You Home. We shall have to hail some passing car to take it into Maidenhead."

Dr. Martineau offered and Sir Richmond took and lit a cigarette.

For a little while conversation hung fire. Then for the first time Dr. Martineau heard his patient laugh.

"Amazing savage!" said Sir Richmond. "Amazing savage!"

He pointed to his handiwork. "The little car looks ruffled. Well it may."

He became grave again. "I suppose I ought to apologize."

Dr. Martineau weighed the situation. "As between doctor and patient," he said. "No."

"Oh!" said Sir Richmond, turned to a new point of view. "But where the patient ends and the host begins. . . . I'm really very sorry."

He reverted to his original train of thought which had not concerned Dr. Martineau at all. "After all, the little car was only doing what she was made to do."

§ 2

The affair of the car effectively unsealed Sir Richmond's mind. Hitherto Dr. Martineau had perceived the possibility and danger of a defensive silence or of a still more defensive irony; but now that Sir Richmond had once given himself away, he seemed prepared to give himself away to an unlimited extent. He embarked upon an apologetic discussion of the choleric temperament.

He began as they stood waiting for the relief car from the Maidenhead garage. "You were talking of the ghosts of apes and monkeys that suddenly come out from the darkness of the subconscious. . . ."

"You mean—when we first met at Harley Street?"

"That last apparition of mine seems to have been a gorilla at least."

The doctor became precise. "Gorillaesque. We are not descended from gorillas."

"Queer thing a fit of rage is!"

"It's one of nature's cruder expedients. Crude, but I doubt if it is fundamental. There doesn't seem to be rage in the vegetable world, and even among the animals——? No, it is not universal." He ran his mind over classes and orders. "Wasps and bees certainly seem to rage, but if one comes to think, most of the invertebrata show very few signs of it."

"I'm not so sure," said Sir Richmond. "I've never seen a snail in a towering passion or an oyster slamming its shell behind it. But these are sluggish things. Oysters sulk, which is after all a smouldering sort of rage. And take any more active invertebrate. Take a spider. Not a smashing and swearing sort of rage perhaps, but a disciplined, cold-blooded malignity. . . . Crabs

fight. . . . A conger eel in a boat will rage—
dangerously."

"A vertebrate. Yes. But even among the verte-
brata; who has ever seen a furious rabbit?"

"Don't the bucks fight?" questioned Sir
Richmond.

Dr. Martineau admitted the point.

"I've always had these fits of passion. As far
back as I can remember. I was a kicking, scream-
ing child. I threw things. I once threw a fork at
my elder brother and it stuck in his forehead,
doing no serious damage—happily. There were
whole days of wrath—days, as I remember them.
Perhaps they were only hours. . . . I've never
thought before what a peculiar thing all this rag-
ing is in the world. *Why* do we rage? They used
to say it was the devil. If it isn't the devil, then
what the devil is it?

"After all," he went on as the doctor was about
to answer his question; "as you pointed out, it
isn't the lowlier things that rage. It's the *higher*
things and *us.*"

"The devil nowadays," the doctor reflected
after a pause, "so far as man is concerned, is
understood to be the ancestral ape. And more
particularly the old male ape."

But Sir Richmond was away on another line
of thought. "Life itself, flaring out. Brooking
no contradiction." He came round suddenly to

the doctor's qualification. "Why male? Don't little girls smash things just as much?"

"They don't," said Dr. Martineau. "Not nearly as much."

Sir Richmond went off at a tangent again. "I suppose you have watched any number of babies?"

"Not nearly as many as a general practitioner would do. There's a lot of rage about most of them at first, male or female."

"Queer little eddies of fury. . . . Recently—it happens—I've been seeing one. A spit of red wrath, clenching its fists and squalling threats at a damned disobedient universe."

The doctor was struck by an idea and glanced quickly and questioningly at his companion's profile.

"Blind driving force," said Sir Richmond, musing.

"Isn't that after all what we really are?" he asked the doctor. "Essentially—Rage. A rage in dead matter, making it alive."

"Schopenhauer," footnoted the doctor. "Boehme."

"Plain fact," said Sir Richmond. "No Rage—no Go."

"But rage without discipline?"

"Discipline afterwards. The rage first."

"But rage against what? And *for* what?"

"Against the Universe. And for——? That's more difficult. What *is* the little beast squalling

itself crimson for? Ultimately? . . . What is it
clutching after? In the long run, what will it
get?"

("Yours the car in distress what sent this?"
asked an unheeded voice.)

"Of course, if you were to say 'desire'," said
Dr. Martineau, "then you would be in line with the
psychoanalysts. They talk of *libido,* meaning a
sort of fundamental desire. Jung speaks of it at
times almost as if it were the universal driving
force."

"No," said Sir Richmond, in love with his new
idea. "Not desire. Desire would have a definite
direction, and that is just what this driving force
hasn't. It's rage."

"Yours the car in distress what sent this?" the
voice repeated. It was the voice of a mechanic
in an Overland car. He was holding up the blue
request for assistance that Sir Richmond had recently filled in.

The two philosophers returned to practical
matters.

§ 3

For half an hour after the departure of the little
Charmeuse car with Sir Richmond and Dr. Martineau, the brass Mercury lay unheeded in the
dusty roadside grass. Then it caught the eye
of a passing child.

He was a bright little boy of five. From the moment when he caught the gleam of brass he knew that he had made the find of his life. But his nurse was a timorous, foolish thing. "You did ought to of left it there, Masterrarry," she said.

"Findings ain't keepings nowadays, not by no manner of means, Masterrarry.

"*Yew*'d look silly if a policeman came along arsting people if they seen a goldennimage.

"Arst yer 'ow you come by it and look pretty straight at you."

All of which grumblings Master Harry treated with an experienced disregard. He knew definitely that he would never relinquish this bright and lovely possession again. It was the first beautiful thing he had ever possessed. He was the darling of fond and indulgent parents and his nursery was crowded with hideous rag and sawdust dolls, golliwogs, comic penguins, comic lions, comic elephants and comic policemen and every variety of suchlike humorous idiocy and visual beastliness. This figure, solid, delicate and gracious, was a thing of a different order.

There was to be much conflict and distress, tears and wrath, before the affinity of that clean-limbed, shining figure and his small soul was recognized. But he carried his point at last. The Mercury became his inseparable darling, his symbol, his private god, the one dignified and serious thing in a little life much congested by the quaint, the burlesque, and all the smiling, dull condescensions of adult love.

CHAPTER THE FOURTH

AT MAIDENHEAD

§ 1

THE little Charmeuse was towed to hospital and
the two psychiatrists took up their quarters at
the Radiant Hotel with its pleasant lawns and
graceful landing stage at the bend towards the
bridge. Sir Richmond, after some trying work
at the telephone, got into touch with his own
proper car. A man would bring that down in two
days' time at latest, and afterwards the detested
coupé could go back to London. The day was
still young, and after lunch and coffee upon a
sunny lawn a boat seemed indicated. Sir Richmond astonished the doctor by going to his room,
reappearing dressed in tennis flannels and looking very well in them. It occurred to the doctor
as a thing hitherto unnoted that Sir Richmond
was not indifferent to his personal appearance.
The doctor had no flannels, but he had brought
a brown holland umbrella lined with green that he
had acquired long ago in Algiers, and this served
to give him something of the riverside quality.

The day was full of sunshine and the river had a
Maytime animation. Pink geraniums, vivid green
lawns, gay awnings, bright glass, white paint and

shining metal set the tone of Maidenhead life. At lunch there had been five or six small tables with quietly affectionate couples who talked in undertones, a tableful of bright-coloured Jews who talked in overtones, and a family party from the Midlands, badly smitten with shyness, who did not talk at all. "A resort of honeymoon couples," said the doctor, and then rather knowingly: "Temporary honeymoons, I fancy, in one or two of the cases."

"Decidedly temporary," said Sir Richmond, considering the company—"in most of the cases anyhow. The two in the corner might be married. You never know nowadays."

He became reflective. . . .

After lunch and coffee he rowed the doctor up the river towards Cliveden.

"The last time I was here," he said, returning to the subject, "I was here on a temporary honeymoon."

The doctor tried to look as though he had not thought that could be possible.

"I know my Maidenhead fairly well," said Sir Richmond. "Aquatic activities, such as rowing, punting, messing about with a boat-hook, tying-up, buzzing about in motor launches, fouling other people's boats, are merely the stage business of the drama. The ruling interests of this place are love—largely illicit— and persistent drinking. . . . Don't you think the bridge charming from here?"

"I shouldn't have thought—*drinking,*" said Dr. Martineau, after he had done justice to the bridge over his shoulder.

"Yes, the place has a floating population of quiet industrious soakers.   The incurable river man and the river girl end at that."

Dr. Martineau encouraged Sir Richmond by an appreciative silence.

"If we are to explore the secret places of the heart," Sir Richmond went on, "we shall have to give some attention to this Maidenhead side of life. It is very material to my case. I have,—as I have said—*been here.* This place has beauty and charm; these piled-up woods behind which my Lords Astor and Desborough keep their state, this shining mirror of the water, brown and green and sky blue, this fringe of reeds and scented rushes and forget-me-not and lilies, and these perpetually posing white swans: they make a picture. A little artificial it is true; one feels the presence of a Conservancy Board, planting the rushes and industriously nicking the swans; but none the less delightful. And this setting has appealed to a number of people as an invitation, as, in a way, a promise.   They come here, responsive to that promise of beauty and happiness. They conceive of themselves here, rowing swiftly and gracefully, punting beautifully, brandishing boat-hooks with ease and charm.   They look to meet, under pleasant or romantic circumstances, other possessors and worshippers of grace and beauty here. There will be glowing evenings, warm moonlight, distant voices singing. . . . There is your desire, doctor, the desire you say is the driving force of life. But reality mocks it. Boats bump and lead to coarse ungracious quarrels; rowing can be curiously fatiguing; punting involves dreadful indignities. The romance here tarnishes very quickly. Romantic encounters fail to occur; in our impatience we resort to—accosting. Chilly mists arise from the water and the magic of distant singing is provided, even excessively, by boatloads of cads—with collecting dishes. When the weather keeps warm there presently arises an extraordinary multitude of gnats, and when it does not there is a need for stimulants. That is why the dreamers who come here first for a light delicious brush with love, come down at last to the Thames-side barmaid with her array of spirits and cordials as the quintessence of all desire.''

''I say,'' said the doctor. ''You tear the place to pieces.''

''The desires of the place,'' said Sir Richmond. ''I'm using the place as a symbol.''

He held his sculls awash, rippling in the water.

''The real force of life, the rage of life, isn't here,'' he said. ''It's down underneath, sulking and smouldering. Every now and then it strains and cracks the surface. This stretch of the Thames, this pleasure stretch, has in fact a curi-

ously quarrelsome atmosphere. People scold and
insult one another for the most trivial things, for
passing too close, for taking the wrong side, for
tying up or floating loose. Most of these notice
boards on the bank show a thoroughly nasty spirit.
People on the banks jeer at anyone in the boats.
You hear people quarreling in boats, in the hotels, as they walk along the towing path. There
is remarkably little happy laughter here. The
rage, you see, is hostile to this place, the *rage*
breaks through. . . . The people who drift from
one pub to another, drinking, the people who fud-
dle in the riverside hotels, are the last fugitives of
pleasure, trying to forget the rage. . . ."

"Isn't it that there is some greater desire at
the back of the human mind?" the doctor suggested. "Which refuses to be content with pleasure as an end?"

"What greater desire?" asked Sir Richmond,
disconcertingly.

"Oh! . . ." The doctor cast about.

"There is no such greater desire," said Sir
Richmond. "You cannot name it. It is just blind
drive. I admit its discontent with pleasure as an
end—but has it any end of its own? At the most
you can say that the rage in life is seeking its
desire and hasn't found it."

"Let us help in the search," said the doctor,
with an afternoon smile under his green umbrella.
"Go on."

§ 2

"Since our first talk in Harley Street," said Sir Richmond, "I have been trying myself over in my mind. (We can drift down this backwater.)"

"Big these trees are," said the doctor with infinite approval.

"I am astonished to discover what a bundle of discordant motives I am. I do not seem to deserve to be called a personality. I cannot discover even a general direction. Much more am I like a taxi-cab in which all sorts of aims and desires have travelled to their destination and got out. Are we all like that?"

"A bundle held together by a name and address and a certain thread of memory?" said the doctor and considered. "More than that. More than that. We have leading ideas, associations, possessions, liabilities."

"We build ourselves a prison of circumstances that keeps us from complete dispersal."

"Exactly," said the doctor. "And there is also something, a consistency, that we call character."

"It changes."

"Consistently with itself."

"I have been trying to recall my sexual history," said Sir Richmond, going off at a tangent. "My sentimental education. I wonder if it differs very widely from yours or most men's."

"Some men are more eventful in these matters than others," said the doctor,—it sounded—wistfully.

"They have the same jumble of motives and traditions, I suspect, whether they are eventful or not. The brakes may be strong or weak but the drive is the same. I can't remember much of the beginnings of curiosity and knowledge in these matters. Can you?"

"Not much," said the doctor. "No."

"Your psychoanalysts tell a story of fears, suppressions, monstrous imaginations, symbolic replacements. I don't remember much of that sort of thing in my own case. It may have faded out of my mind. There were probably some uneasy curiosities, a grotesque dream or so perhaps; I can't recall anything of that sort distinctly now. I had a very lively interest in women, even when I was still quite a little boy, and a certain—what shall I call it?—imaginative slavishness—not towards actual women but towards something magnificently feminine. My first love——"

Sir Richmond smiled at some secret memory. "My first love was Britannia as depicted by Tenniel in the cartoons in *Punch*. I must have been a very little chap at the time of the Britannia affair. I just clung to her in my imagination and did devoted things for her. Then I recall, a little later, a secret abject adoration for the white goddesses of the Crystal Palace. Not for any particular one

of them that I can remember,—for all of them.
But I don't remember anything very monstrous
or incestuous in my childish imaginations,—such
things as Freud, I understand, lays stress upon.
If there was an Œdipus complex or anything of
that sort in my case it has been very completely
washed out again. Perhaps a child which is
brought up in a proper nursery of its own and sees
a lot of pictures of the nude human body, and so
on, gets its mind shifted off any possible concentration upon—the domestic aspect of sex. I got
to definite knowledge pretty early. By the time I
was eleven or twelve."

"Normally?"

"What is normally? Decently, anyhow. Here
again I may be forgetting much secret and shameful curiosity. I got my ideas into definite form
out of a little straightforward physiological teaching and some dissecting of rats and mice. My
schoolmaster was a capable sane man in advance
of his times and my people believed in him. I
think much of this distorted perverse stuff that
grows up in people's minds about sex and de-
velops into evil vices and still more evil habits,
is due to the mystery we make about these things."

"Not entirely," said the doctor.

"Largely. What child under a modern up-
bringing ever goes through the stuffy horrors described in James Joyce's *Portrait of the Author
as a Young Man?*"

"I've not read it."

"A picture of the Catholic atmosphere; a young soul shut up in darkness and ignorance to accumulate filth. In the name of purity and decency and under threats of hell fire."

"Horrible!"

"Quite. A study of intolerable tensions, the tensions that make young people write unclean words in secret places."

"Yes, we certainly ventilate and sanitate in those matters nowadays. Where nothing is concealed, nothing can explode."

"On the whole I came up to adolescence pretty straight and clean," said Sir Richmond. "What stands out in my memory now is this idea of a sort of woman goddess who was very lovely and kind and powerful and wonderful. That ruled my secret imaginations as a boy, but it was very much in my mind as I grew up."

"The mother complex," said Dr. Martineau as a passing botanist might recognize and name a flower.

Sir Richmond stared at him for a moment.

"It had not the slightest connexion with my mother or any mother or any particular woman at all. Far better to call it the goddess complex."

"The connexion is not perhaps immediately visible," said the doctor.

"There was no connexion," said Sir Richmond. "The women of my adolescent dreams were stripped and strong and lovely. They were great creatures. They came, it was clearly traceable, from pictures, sculpture—and from a definite response in myself to their beauty. My mother had nothing whatever to do with that. The women and girls about me were fussy bunches of clothes that I am sure I never even linked with that dream world of love and worship.''

''Were you co-educated?''

''No. But I had a couple of sisters, one older, one younger than myself, and there were plenty of girls in my circle. I thought some of them pretty—but that was a different affair. I know that I didn't connect them with the idea of the loved and worshipped goddesses at all, because I remember when I first saw the goddess in a real human being and how amazed I was at the discovery. . . . I was a boy of twelve or thirteen. My people took me one summer to Dymchurch in Romney Marsh; in those days before the automobile had made the Marsh accessible to the Hythe and Folkestone crowds, it was a little old forgotten silent wind-bitten village crouching under the lee of the great sea wall. At low water there were miles of sand as smooth and shining as the skin of a savage brown woman. Shining and with a texture—the very same. And one day as I was mucking about by myself on the beach, boy fashion,—there were some ribs of a wrecked boat buried in the sand near a groin and I was busy with them—a girl ran out from a tent high up on the beach and across the sands to the water. She was dressed in a tight bathing dress and not in the clumsy skirts and frills that it was the custom to inflict on women in those days. Her hair was tied up in a blue handkerchief. She ran swiftly and gracefully, intent upon the white line of foam ahead. I can still remember how the sunlight touched her round neck and cheek as she went past me. She was the loveliest, most shapely thing I have ever seen—to this day. She lifted up her arms and thrust through the dazzling white and green breakers and plunged into the water and swam; she swam straight out for a long way as it seemed to me, and presently came in and passed me again on her way back to her tent, light and swift and sure. The very prints of her feet on the sand were beautiful. Suddenly I realized that there could be living people in the world as lovely as any goddess. . . . She wasn't in the least out of breath.

"That was my first human love. And I love that girl still. I doubt sometimes whether I have ever loved anyone else. I kept the thing very secret. I wonder now why I have kept the thing so secret. Until now I have never told a soul about it. I resorted to all sorts of tortuous devices and excuses to get a chance of seeing her again without betraying what it was I was after."

Dr. Martineau retained a simple fondness for a story.

"And did you meet her again?"

"Never. Of course I may have seen her as a dressed-up person and not recognized her. A day or so later I was stabbed to the heart by the discovery that the tent she came out of had been taken away."

"She had gone?"

"For ever."

Sir Richmond smiled brightly at the doctor's disappointment.

§ 3

"I was never wholehearted and simple about sexual things," Sir Richmond resumed presently. "Never. I do not think any man is. We are too much plastered-up things, too much the creatures of a tortuous and complicated evolution."

Dr. Martineau, under his green umbrella, nodded his conceded agreement.

"This—what shall I call it?—this Dream of Women, grew up in my mind as I grew up—as something independent of and much more important than the reality of Women. It came only very slowly into relation with that. That girl on the Dymchurch beach was one of the first links, but she ceased very speedily to be real—she joined the women of dreamland at last altogether. She became a sort of legendary incarnation. I thought of these dream women not only as something beautiful but as something exceedingly kind and helpful. The girls and women I met belonged to a different creation. . . ."

Sir Richmond stopped abruptly and rowed a few long strokes.

Dr. Martineau sought information.

"I suppose," he said, "there was a sensuous element in these dreamings?"

"Certainly. A very strong one. It didn't dominate but it was a very powerful undertow."

"Was there any tendency in all this imaginative stuff to concentrate? To group itself about a single figure, the sort of thing that Victorians would have called an ideal?"

"Not a bit of it," said Sir Richmond with conviction. "There was always a tremendous lot of variety in my mind. In fact the thing I liked least in the real world was the way it was obsessed by the idea of pairing off with one particular set and final person. I liked to dream of a blonde goddess in her own Venusberg one day, and the next I would be off over the mountains with an armed Brunhild."

"You had little thought of children?"

"As a young man?"

"Yes."

"None at all. I cannot recall a single philopro-genitive moment. These dream women were all conceived of, and I was conceived of, as being concerned in some tremendous enterprise—something quite beyond domesticity. It kept us related— gave us dignity. . . . Certainly it wasn't babies.''

"All this is very interesting, very interesting, from the scientific point of view. *A priori* it is not what one might have expected. Reasoning from the idea that all instincts and natural imaginations are adapted to a biological end and seeing that sex is essentially a method of procreation, one might reasonably expect a convergence, if not a complete concentration, upon the idea of offspring. It is almost as if there were other ends to be served. It is clear that Nature has not worked this impulse out to any sight of its end. Has not perhaps troubled to do so. The instinct of the male for the female isn't primarily for offspring—not even in the most intelligent and farseeing types. The desire just points to glowing satisfactions and illusions. Quite equally I think the desire of the female for the male ignores its end. Nature has set about this business in a *cheap* sort of way. She is like some pushful advertising tradesman. She isn't frank with us; she just humbugs us into what she wants with us. All very well in the early Stone Age—when the poor dear things never realized that their mutual endearments meant all the troubles and responsibilities of parentage. But *now*——!''

He shook his head sideways and twirled the green umbrella like an animated halo around his large broad-minded face.

Sir Richmond considered. "Desire has never been the chief incentive of my relations with women. Never. So far as I can analyze the thing, it has been a craving for a particular sort of life-giving companionship."

"That I take it is Nature's device to keep the lovers together in the interest of the more or less unpremeditated offspring."

"A poor device, if that is its end. It doesn't keep parents together; more often it tears them apart. The wife or the mistress, so soon as she is encumbered with children, becomes all too manifestly *not* the companion goddess. . . ."

Sir Richmond brooded over his sculls and thought.

"Throughout my life I have been an exceedingly busy man. I have done a lot of scientific work and some of it has been very good work. And very laborious work. I've travelled much. I've organized great business developments. You might think that my time has been fairly well filled without much philandering. And all the time, all the time, I've been—about women—like a thirsty beast looking for water. . . . Always. Always. All through my life."

Dr. Martineau waited through another silence.

"I was very grave about it at first. I married

young. I married very simply and purely. I was
not one of those young men who sow a large crop
of wild oats. I was a fairly decent youth. It suddenly appeared to me that a certain smiling and
dainty girl could make herself into all the goddesses of my dreams. I had but to win her and
this miracle would occur. Of course I forget now
the exact things I thought and felt then, but surely
I had some such persuasion. Or why should I
have married her? My wife was seven years
younger than myself, a girl of twenty. She was
charming. She *is* charming. She is a wonderfully
intelligent and understanding woman. She has
made a home for me—a delightful home. I am one
of those men who have no instinct for home making. I owe my home and all the comfort and dignity of my life to her ability. I have no excuse for
any misbehaviour—so far as she is concerned.
None at all. By all the rules I should have been
completely happy. But instead of my marriage
satisfying me, it presently released a storm of
long-controlled desires and imprisoned cravings.
A voice within me became more and more urgent.
'This will not do. This is not love. Where are
your goddesses? This is not love.' . . . And I
was unfaithful to my wife within four years of my
marriage. It was a sudden overpowering impulse.
But I suppose the ground had been preparing for
a long time. I forget now all the emotions of that
adventure. I suppose at the time it seemed beau-

tiful and wonderful. . . . I do not excuse myself. Still less do I condemn myself. I put the facts before you. So it was.''

"There were no children by your marriage?''

"Your line of thought, doctor, is too philopro-genitive. We have had three. My daughter was married two years ago. She is in America. One little boy died when he was three. The other is in India, taking up the Mardipore power scheme again now that he is out of the army. . . . No, it is simply that I was hopelessly disappointed with everything that a good woman and a decent marriage had to give me. Pure disappointment and vexation. The anti-climax to an immense expectation built up throughout an imaginative boyhood and youth and early manhood. I was shocked and ashamed at my own disappointment. I thought it mean and base. Nevertheless this orderly household into which I had placed my life, these almost methodical connubialities . . .''

He broke off in mid-sentence.

Dr. Martineau shook his head disapprovingly.

"No," he said, "it wasn't fair to your wife.''

"It was shockingly unfair. I have always realized that. I've done what I could to make things up to her. . . . Heaven knows what counter disappointments she has concealed. . . . But it is no good arguing about rights and wrongs now. This is not an apology for my life. I am telling you what happened.''

"Not for me to judge," said Dr. Martineau. "Go on."

"By marrying I had got nothing that my soul craved for, I had satisfied none but the most transitory desires and I had incurred a tremendous obligation. That obligation didn't restrain me from making desperate lunges at something vaguely beautiful that I felt was necessary to me; but it did cramp and limit these lunges. So my story flops down into the comedy of the lying, cramped intrigues of a respectable, married man. I was still driven by my dream of some extravagantly beautiful inspiration called love and I sought it like an area sneak. Gods! What a story it is when one brings it all together! I couldn't believe that the glow and sweetness I dreamt of were not in the world—somewhere. Hidden away from me. I seemed to catch glimpses of the dear lost thing, now in the corners of a smiling mouth, now in dark eyes beneath a black smoke of hair, now in a slim form seen against the sky. Often I cared nothing for the woman I made love to. I cared for the thing she seemed to be hiding from me. . . ."

Sir Richmond's voice altered.

"I don't see what possible good it can do to talk over these things." He began to row and rowed perhaps a score of strokes. Then he stopped and the boat drove on with a whisper of water at the bow and over the outstretched oar blades.

"What a muddle and mockery the whole thing is!" he cried. "What a fumbling old fool old Mother Nature has been! She drives us into indignity and dishonour: and she doesn't even get the children which are her only excuse for her mischief. See what a fantastic thing I am when you take the machine to pieces! I have been a busy and responsible man throughout my life. I have handled complicated public and industrial affairs not unsuccessfully and discharged quite big obligations fully and faithfully. And all the time, hidden away from the public eye, my life has been laced by the thread of these—what can one call them? —love adventures. How many? you ask. I don't know. Never have I been a whole-hearted lover; never have I been able to leave love alone. . . . Never has love left me alone.

"And as I am made," said Sir Richmond with sudden insistence, *"as I am made*—I do not believe that I could go on without these affairs. I know that you will be disposed to dispute that."

Dr. Martineau made a reassuring noise.

"These affairs are at once unsatisfying and vitally necessary. It is only latterly that I have begun to perceive this. Women *make* life for me. Whatever they touch or see or desire becomes worth while and otherwise it is not worth while. Whatever is lovely in my world, whatever is delightful, has been so conveyed to me by some woman. Without the vision they give me, I should be a hard dry industry in the world, a worker ant, a soulless rage, making much, valuing nothing.''

He paused.

''You are, I think, abnormal,'' considered the doctor.

''Not abnormal. Excessive, if you like. Without women I am a wasting fever of distressful toil. Without them there is no kindness in existence, no rest, no sort of satisfaction. The world is a battlefield, trenches, barbed wire, rain, mud, logical necessity and utter desolation—with nothing whatever worth fighting for. Whatever justifies effort, whatever restores energy is hidden in women. . . .''

''An access of sex,'' said Dr. Martineau. ''This is a phase. . . .''

''It is how I am made,'' said Sir Richmond.

A brief silence fell upon that. Dr. Martineau persisted. ''It isn't how you are made. We are getting to something in all this. It is, I insist, a *mood* of how you are made. A distinctive and indicative mood.''

Sir Richmond went on, almost as if he soliloquized.

''I would go through it all again. . . . There are times when the love of women seems the only real thing in the world to me. And always it remains the most real thing. I do not know how far I may be a normal man or how far I may not be, so to speak, abnormally male, but to me life

has very little personal significance and no value
or power until it has a woman as intermediary.
Before life can talk to me and say anything that
matters a woman must be present as a medium.
I don't mean that it has no significance mentally
and logically; I mean that irrationally and emotionally it has no significance. Works of art, for
example, bore me, literature bores me, scenery
bores me, even the beauty of a woman bores me,
unless I find in it some association with a woman's
feeling. It isn't that I can't tell for myself that
a picture is fine or a mountain valley lovely, but
that it doesn't matter a rap to me whether it is or
whether it isn't until there is a feminine response,
a sexual motif, if you like to call it that, coming in.
Whatever there is of loveliness or pride in life
doesn't *live* for me until somehow a woman comes
in and breathes upon it the breath of life. I cannot even rest until a woman makes holiday for me.
Only one thing can I do without women and that is
work, joylessly but effectively, and latterly for
some reason that it is up to you to discover, doctor, even the power of work has gone from me.

§ 4

"This afternoon brings back to me very vividly
my previous visit here. It was perhaps a dozen or
fifteen years ago. We rowed down this same

backwater. I can see my companion's hand—she had very pretty hands with rosy palms—trailing in the water, and her shadowed face smiling quietly under her sunshade, with little faint streaks of sunlight, reflected from the ripples, dancing and quivering across it. She was one of those people who seem always to be happy and to radiate happiness.

"By ordinary standards," said Sir Richmond, "she was a thoroughly bad lot. She had about as much morality, in the narrower sense of the word, as a monkey. And yet she stands out in my mind as one of the most honest women I have ever met. She was certainly one of the kindest. Part of that effect of honesty may have been due to her open brow, her candid blue eyes, the smiling frankness of her manner. . . . But—no! She was really honest.

"We drifted here as we are doing now. She pulled at the sweet rushes and crushed them in her hand. She adds a remembered brightness to this afternoon.

"Honest. Friendly. Of all the women I have known, this woman who was here with me came nearest to being my friend. You know, what we call virtue in a woman is a tremendous handicap to any real friendliness with a man. Until she gets to an age when virtue and fidelity are no longer urgent practical concerns, a good woman, by the very definition of feminine goodness, isn't truly herself. Over a vast extent of her being she is *reserved*. She suppresses a vast amount of her being, holds back, denies, hides. On the other hand, there is a frankness and honesty in openly bad women arising out of the admitted fact that they are bad, that they hide no treasure from you, they have no peculiarly precious and delicious secrets to keep, and no poverty to conceal. Intellectually they seem to be more manly and vigorous because they are, as people say, unsexed. Many old women, thoroughly respectable old women, have the same quality. Because they have gone out of the personal sex business. Haven't you found that?"

"I have never," said the doctor, "known what you call an openly bad woman,—at least, at all intimately. . . ."

Sir Richmond looked with quick curiosity at his companion. "You have avoided them?"

"They don't attract me."

"They repel you?"

"For me," said the doctor, "for any friendliness, a woman must be modest. . . . My habits of thought are old-fashioned, I suppose, but the mere suggestion about a woman that there were no barriers, no reservation, that in any fashion she might more than meet me half way . . ."

His facial expression completed his sentence.

"Now I wonder," whispered Sir Richmond, and hesitated for a moment before he carried the great research into the explorer's country. "You are afraid of women?" he said, with a smile to mitigate the impertinence.

"I respect them."

"An element of fear."

"Well, I am afraid of them then. Put it that way if you like. Anyhow I do not let myself go with them. I have never let myself go."

"You lose something. You lose a reality of insight."

There was a thoughtful interval.

"Having found so excellent a friend," said the doctor, "why did you ever part from her?"

Sir Richmond seemed indisposed to answer, but Dr. Martineau's face remained slantingly interrogative. He had found the effective counterattack and he meant to press it.

"I was jealous of her," Sir Richmond admitted. "I couldn't stand that side of it."

§ 5

After a meditative silence the doctor became briskly professional again.

"You care for your wife," he said. "You care very much for your wife. She is, as you say, your great obligation and you are a man to respect obligations. I grasp that. Then you tell me of these women who have come and gone. . . . About them too you are perfectly frank. . . . There remains someone else."

Sir Richmond stared at his physician.

"Well," he said and laughed. "I didn't pretend to have made my autobiography anything more than a sketch."

"No, but there is a special person, the current person."

"I haven't dilated on my present situation, I admit."

"From some little things that have dropped from you, I should say there is a child."

"That," said Sir Richmond after a brief pause, "is a good guess."

"Not older than three."

"Two years and a half."

"You and this lady who is, I guess, young, are separated. At any rate, you can't go to her. That leaves you at loose ends, because for some time, for two or three years at least, you have ceased to be—how shall I put it?—an emotional wanderer."

"I begin to respect your psychoanalysis."

"Hence your overwhelming sense of the necessity of feminine companionship for weary men. I guess she is a very jolly companion to be with, amusing, restful—interesting."

"H'm," said Sir Richmond. "I think that is a fair description. When she cares, that is. When she is in good form."

"Which she isn't at present," hazarded the doctor.

He exploded a mine of long-pent exasperation. "She is the clumsiest hand at keeping well that I have ever known. Health is a woman's primary duty. But she is incapable of the most elementary precautions. She is maddeningly receptive to every infection. At the present moment, when I am ill, when I am in urgent need of help and happiness, she has let that wretched child get measles and she herself won't let me go near her because she has got something disfiguring, something nobody else could ever have or think of having, called *carbuncle*. Carbuncle!"

"It is very painful," said Dr. Martineau.

"No doubt it is," said Sir Richmond. "No doubt it is." His voice grew bitter. He spoke with deliberation. "A perfectly aimless, useless illness,—and as painful as it *can* be."

He spoke as if he slammed a door viciously. And indeed he had slammed a door. The doctor realized that for the present there was no more self-dissection to be got from Sir Richmond.

For some time Sir Richmond had been keeping the boat close up to the foaming weir to the left of the lock by an occasional stroke. Now with a general air of departure he swung the boat round and began to row down stream towards the bridge and the Radiant Hotel.

"Time we had tea," he said.

§ 6

After tea Dr. Martineau left Sir Richmond in a chair upon the lawn, brooding darkly—apparently over the crime of the carbuncle. The doctor went to his room, ostensibly to write a couple of letters and put on a dinner jacket, but really to make a few notes of the afternoon's conversation and meditate over his impressions while they were fresh.

His room proffered a comfortable armchair and into this he sank. . . . A number of very discrepant things were busy in his mind. He had experienced a disconcerting personal attack. There was a whirl of active resentment in the confusion.

"Apologetics of a rake," he tried presently.

"A common type, stripped of his intellectual dressing. Every third manufacturer from the midlands or the north has some such undertow of 'affairs.' A physiological uneasiness, an imaginative laxity, the temptations of the trip to London—weakness masquerading as a psychological necessity. The Lady of the Carbuncle seems to have got rather a hold upon him. She has kept him in order for three or four years."

The doctor scrutinized his own remarks with a judicious expression.

"I am not being fair. He ruffled me. Even if it is true, as I said, that every third manufac-

turer from the midlands is in much the same case
as he is, that does not dismiss the case. It makes
it a more important one, much more important: it
makes it a type case with the exceptional quality
of being self-expressive. . . . Almost too self-
expressive.

"Sir Richmond does, after all, make out a sort
of case for himself. . . .

"A valid case?"

The doctor sat deep in his chair, frowning judicially with the fingers of one hand apposed to the
fingers of the other. "He makes me bristle because all his life and ideas challenge my way
of living. . . . But if I eliminate the personal
element?"

He pulled a sheet of note-paper towards him
and began to jot down notes with a silver-cased
pencil. Soon he discontinued writing and sat tap-
ping his pencil-case on the table.

"The amazing selfishness of his attitude! I do
not think that once—not once—has he judged any
woman except as a contributor to his energy and
peace of mind. . . . Except in the case of his
wife. . . .

"For her his habit of respect was formed before his ideas developed. . . .

"That I think explains *her*. . . .

"What was his phrase about the unfortunate
young woman with the carbuncle? . . . 'Totally
useless and unnecessary illness,' was it? . . .

"Now has a man any right by any standards to use women as this man has used them?

"By any standards?"

The doctor frowned and nodded his head slowly with the corners of his mouth drawn in.

For some years now an intellectual reverie had been playing an increasing part in the good doctor's life. He was writing this book of his, writing it very deliberately and laboriously, *The Psychology of a New Age,* but much more was he dreaming and thinking about this book. Its publication was to mark an epoch in human thought and human affairs generally, and create a considerable flutter of astonishment in the doctor's own little world. It was to bring home to people some various aspects of one very startling proposition: that human society had arrived at a phase when the complete restatement of its fundamental ideas had become urgently necessary, a phase when the slow, inadequate, partial adjustments to two centuries of changing conditions had to give place to a rapid reconstruction of new fundamental ideas. And it was a fact of great value in the drama of these secret dreams that the directive force towards this fundamentally reconstructed world should be the pen of an unassuming Harley Street physician, hitherto not suspected of any great excesses of enterprise.

The written portions of this book were already in a highly polished state. They combined a limit-

less freedom of proposal with a smooth urbanity
of manner, a tacit denial that the thoughts of one
intelligent being could possibly be shocking to
another. Upon this the doctor was very insistent.
Conduct, he held, could never be sufficiently discreet, thought could never be sufficiently free. As
a citizen one had to treat a law or an institution
as a thing as rigidly right as a natural law. That
the social well-being demands. But as a scientific
man, in one's stated thoughts and in public discussion, the case was altogether different. There
was no offence in any possible hypothesis or in the
contemplation of any possibility. Just as when
one played a game one was bound to play in un-
questioning obedience to the laws and spirit of the
game, but if one was not playing that game then
there was no reason why one should not contem-
plate the completest reversal of all its methods
and the alteration and abandonment of every rule.
Correctness of conduct, the doctor held, was an
imperative concomitant of all really free thinking.
Revolutionary speculation is one of those things
that must be divorced absolutely from revolutionary conduct. It was to the neglect of these ob-
vious principles, as the doctor considered them,
that the general muddle in contemporary marital
affairs was very largely due. We left divorce-law
revision to exposed adulterers and marriage re-
form to hot adolescents and craving spinsters
driven by the furies within them to assertions that

established nothing and to practical demonstrations that only left everybody thoroughly uncomfortable. Far better to leave all these matters to calm, patient men in easy chairs, weighing typical cases impartially, ready to condone, indisposed to envy.

In return for which restraint on the part of the eager and adventurous, the calm patient man was prepared in his thoughts to fly high and go far. Without giving any guarantee, of course, that he might not ultimately return to the comfortable point of inaction from which he started.

In Sir Richmond, Dr. Martineau found the most interesting and encouraging confirmation of the fundamental idea of *The Psychology of a New Age,* the immediate need of new criteria of conduct altogether. Here was a man whose life was evidently ruled by standards that were at once very high and very generous. He was overworking himself to the pitch of extreme distress and apparently he was doing this for ends that were essentially unselfish. Manifestly there were many things that an ordinary industrial or political magnate would do that Sir Richmond would not dream of doing, and a number of things that such a man would not feel called upon to do that he would regard as imperative duties. And mixed up with so much fine intention and fine conduct was this disreputable streak of intrigue and this ex-

traordinary claim that such misconduct was
necessary to continued vigour of action.

"To energy of thought it is *not* necessary," said
Dr. Martineau, and considered for a time.

"Yet—certainly—I am not a man of action. I
admit it. I make few decisions."

The chapters of the *Psychology of a New Age*
dealing with women were still undrafted, but they
had already greatly exercised the doctor's mind.
He found now that the case of Sir Richmond had
stirred his imagination. He sat with his hands
apposed, his head on one side, and an expression
of great intellectual contentment on his face while
these emancipated ideas gave a sort of gala per-
formance in his mind.

The good doctor did not dislike women, he had
always guarded himself very carefully against
misogyny, but he was very strongly disposed to
regard them as much less necessary in the existing
scheme of things than was generally assumed.
Women, he conceded, had laid the foundations of
social life. Through their contrivances and sacrifices and patience the fierce and lonely patriarchal
family-herd of a male and his women and offspring had grown into the clan and tribe; the
woven tissue of related families that constitute
the human comity had been woven by the subtle,
persistent protection of sons and daughters by
their mothers against the intolerant, jealous, pos-
sessive Old Man. But that was a thing of the re-

mote past. Little was left of those ancient struggles now but a few infantile dreams and nightmares. The greater human community, human society, was made for good. And being made, it had taken over the ancient tasks of the woman, one by one, until now in its modern forms it cherished more sedulously than she did, it educated, it housed and comforted, it clothed and served and nursed, leaving the wife privileged, honoured, protected, for the sake of tasks she no longer did and of a burthen she no longer bore. "Progress has *trivialized* women," said the doctor, and made a note of the word for later consideration.

"And woman has trivialized civilization," the doctor tried.

"She has retained her effect of being central, she still makes the social atmosphere, she raises men's instinctive hopes of help and direction. Except," the doctor stipulated, "for a few highly developed modern types, most men found the sense of achieving her a necessary condition for sustained exertion. And there is no direction in her any more.

"She spends," said the doctor, "she just spends. She spends excitingly and competitively for her own pride and glory, she drives all the energy of men over the weirs of gain. . . .

"What are we to do with the creature?" whispered the doctor.

Apart from the procreative necessity, was woman an unavoidable evil? The doctor's untrammelled thoughts began to climb high, spin, nose dive and loop the loop. Nowadays we took a proper care of the young, we had no need for high birth rates, quite a small proportion of women with a gift in that direction could supply all the offspring that the world wanted. Given the power of determining sex that science was slowly winning to-day, and why should we have so many women about? A drastic elimination of the creatures would be quite practicable. A fantastic world to a vulgar imagination, no doubt, but to a calmly reasonable mind by no means fantastic. But this was where the case of Sir Richmond became so interesting. Was it really true that the companionship of women was necessary to these energetic creative types? Was it the fact that the drive of life towards action, as distinguished from contemplation, arose out of sex and needed to be refreshed by the reiteration of that motive? It was a plausible proposition: it marched with all the doctor's ideas of natural selection and of the conditions of a survival that have made us what we are. It was in tune with the Freudian analyses.

"Sex not only a renewal of life in the species," noted the doctor's silver pencil; *"sex may be also a renewal of energy in the individual."*

After some musing he crossed out "sex" and wrote above it "sexual love."

"That is practically what he claims," Dr. Martineau said. "In which case we want the completest revision of all our standards of sexual obligation. We want a new system of restrictions and imperatives altogether."

It was a fixed idea of the doctor's that women were quite incapable of producing ideas in the same way that men do, but he believed that with suitable encouragement they could be induced to respond quite generously to such ideas. Suppose therefore we really educated the imaginations of women; suppose we turned their indubitable capacity for service towards social and political creativeness, not in order to make them the rivals of men in these fields, but their moral and actual helpers.

"A man of this sort wants a mistress-mother," said the doctor. "He wants a sort of woman who cares more for him and his work and honour than she does for child or home or clothes or personal pride.

"But are there such women?

"Can there be such a woman?

"His work needs to be very fine to deserve her help. But admitting its fineness? . . .

"The alternative seems to be to teach the sexes to get along without each other.

"A neutralized world. A separated world.

The darkness concealed a faint smile on the doctor's face.

"The work is the thing," said Sir Richmond. "So long as one can keep one's grip on it."

"What," said the doctor after a pause, leaning back and sending wreaths of smoke up towards the star-dusted zenith, "what is your idea of your work? I mean, how do you see it in relation to yourself—and things generally?"

"Put in the most general terms?"

"Put in the most general terms."

"I wonder if I can put it in general terms for you at all. It is hard to put something one is always thinking about in general terms or to think of it as a whole. . . . Now. . . . Fuel? . . .

"I suppose it was my father's business interests that pushed me towards specialization in fuel. He wanted me to have a thoroughly scientific training in days when a scientific training was less easy to get for a boy than it is to-day. And much more inspiring when you got it. My mind was framed, so to speak, in geology and astronomical physics. I grew up to think on that scale. Just as a man who has been trained in history and law grows to think on the scale of the Roman empire. I don't know what your pocket map of the universe is,—the map, I mean, by which you judge all sorts of other general ideas. To me this planet is a little ball of oxides and nickel steel; life a sort of tarnish on its surface. And we,—the mi-

nutest particles in that tarnish. Who can nevertheless, in some unaccountable way, take in the
idea of this universe as one whole,—who begin to
dream of taking control of it.''

''That is not a bad statement of the scientific
point of view. I suppose I have much the same
general idea of the world. On rather more psychological lines.''

''We think, I suppose,'' said Sir Richmond, ''of
life as something that is only just beginning to be
aware of what it is—and what it might be.''

''Exactly,'' said the doctor. ''Good.''

He went on eagerly. ''That is precisely how I
see it. You and I are just particles in the tarnish,
as you call it, who are becoming dimly awake to
what we are, to what we have in common. Only
a very few of us have got as far even as this. . . .
These others here, for example. . . .''

He indicated the rest of Maidenhead by a
movement.

''Desire, mutual flattery, egotistical dreams,
greedy solicitudes fill them up. They haven't begun to get out of themselves.''

''We, I suppose, have,'' doubted Sir Richmond.

''We have.''

The doctor had no doubt. He lay back in his
chair, with his hands behind his head and his
smoke ascending vertically to heaven. With the
greatest contentment he began quoting himself.
''This getting out of one's individuality—this con-

scious getting out of one's individuality—is one of the most important and interesting aspects of the psychology of the new age that is now dawning. As compared with any previous age. Unconsciously, of course, every true artist, every philosopher, every scientific investigator, so far as his art or thought went, has always got out of himself,—has forgotten his personal interests and become Man thinking for the whole race. And intimations of the same thing have been at the heart of most religions. But now people are beginning to get this detachment without any distinctively religious feeling or any distinctive æsthetic or intellectual impulse, as if it were a plain matter of fact. Plain matter of fact,—that we are only incidentally ourselves. That really each one of us is also the whole species, is really indeed all life."

"A part of it."

"An integral part—as sight is part of a man . . . with no absolute separation from all the rest —no more than a separation of the imagination. The whole so far as his distinctive quality goes. I do not know how this takes shape in your mind, Sir Richmond, but to me this idea of actually being life itself upon the world, a special phase of it dependent upon and connected with all other phases, and of being one of a small but growing number of people who apprehend that, and want to live in the spirit of that, is quite central. It is

my fundamental idea. We,—this small but growing minority—constitute that part of life which
knows and wills and tries to rule its destiny. This
new realization, the new psychology arising out of
it, is a fact of supreme importance in the history of
life. It is like the appearance of self-consciousness in some creature that has not hitherto had
self-consciousness. And so far as we are concerned, we are the true kingship of the world.
Necessarily. We who know, are the true king.
. . . I wonder how this appeals to you. It is stuff
I have thought out very slowly and carefully and
written and approved. It is the very core of my
life. . . . And yet when one comes to say these
things to someone else, face to face. . . . It is
much more difficult to say than to write.''

Sir Richmond noted how the doctor's chair
creaked as he rolled to and fro with the uneasiness
of these intimate utterances.

''I agree,'' said Sir Richmond presently. ''One
does think in this fashion. Something in this fashion. What one calls one's work does belong to
something much bigger than ourselves.

''Something much bigger,'' he expanded.

''Which something we become,'' the doctor urged, ''in so far as our work takes hold
of us.''

Sir Richmond made no answer to this for a little while. ''Of course we trail a certain egotism
into our work,'' he said.

"Could we do otherwise? But it has ceased to be purely egotism. It is no longer, 'I am I' but 'I am part.' . . . One wants to be an honourable part."

"You think of man upon his planet," the doctor pursued. "I think of life rather as a mind that tries itself over in millions and millions of trials. But it works out to the same thing."

"I think in terms of fuel," said Sir Richmond. He was still debating the doctor's generalization. "I suppose it would be true to say that I think of myself as mankind on his planet, with very considerable possibilities and with only a limited amount of fuel at his disposal to achieve them. Yes. . . . I agree that I think in that way. . . . I have not thought much before of the way in which I think about things—but I agree that it is in that way. Whatever enterprises mankind attempts are limited by the sum total of that store of fuel upon the planet. That is very much in my mind. Besides that he has nothing but his annual allowance of energy from the sun."

"I thought that presently we were to get un-limited energy from atoms," said the doctor.

"I don't believe in that as a thing immediately practicable. No doubt getting a supply of energy from atoms is a theoretical possibility,—just as flying was in the time of Dædalus; probably there were actual attempts at some sort of glider in ancient Crete. But before we get to the actual

utilization of atomic energy there will be ten thousand difficult corners to turn; we may have to wait
three or four thousand years for it. We cannot
count on it. We haven't it in hand. There may
be some impasse. All we have surely is coal and
oil,—there is no surplus of wood now—only an
annual growth. And water-power is income also,
doled out day by day. We cannot anticipate it.
Coal and oil are our only capital. They are all
we have for great important efforts. They are
a gift to mankind to use to some supreme end or
to waste in trivialities. Coal is the key to metal-
lurgy and oil to transit. When they are done we
shall either have built up such a fabric of apparatus, knowledge and social organization that
we shall be able to manage without them—or
we shall have travelled a long way down the
slopes of waste towards extinction. . . . To-day,
in getting, in distribution, in use we waste enormously. . . . As we sit here all the world is wasting fuel—fantastically.''

"Just as mentally—educationally we waste,''
the doctor interjected.

"And my job is to stop what I can of that waste,
to do what I can to organize, first of all sane fuel
getting and then sane fuel using. And that second
proposition carries us far. Into the whole use
we are making of life.

"First things first,'' said Sir Richmond. "If
we set about getting fuel sanely, if we do it as the

deliberate, co-operative act of the whole species,
then it follows that we shall look very closely into
the use that is being made of it. When all the fuel
getting is brought into one view as a common interest, then it follows that all the fuel burning will
be brought into one view. At present we are getting fuel in a kind of scramble with no general aim.
We waste and lose almost as much as we get. And
of what we get, the waste is idiotic.

"I won't trouble you," said Sir Richmond,
"with any long discourse on the ways of getting
fuel in this country. But land as you know is
owned in patches and stretches that were determined in the first place chiefly by agricultural
necessities. When it was divided up among its
present owners nobody was thinking about the
minerals beneath. But the lawyers settled long
ago that the landowner owned his land right down
to the centre of the earth. So we have the superficial landlord as coal owner trying to work his
coal according to the superficial divisions, quite
irrespective of the lie of the coal underneath.
Each man goes for the coal under his own land
in his own fashion. You get three shafts where
one would suffice and none of them in the best possible place. You get the coal coming out of this
point when it would be far more convenient to
bring it out at that—miles away. You get bound-
ary walls of coal between the estates, abandoned,
left in the ground for ever. And each coal owner

sells his coal in his own pettifogging manner. . . .
But you know of these things. You know too how
we trail the coal all over the country, spoiling
it as we trail it, until at last we get it into the
silly coal scuttles beside the silly, wasteful, air-
poisoning, fog-creating fireplace.

"And this stuff," said Sir Richmond, bringing
his hand down so smartly on the table that the
startled coffee cups cried out upon the tray; "was
given to men to give them power over metals, to
get knowledge with, to get more power with. . . ."

"The oil story, I suppose, is as bad."

"The oil story is worse. . . .

"There is a sort of cant," said Sir Richmond
in a fierce parenthesis, "that the supplies of oil
are inexhaustible—that you can muddle about
with oil anyhow. . . . Optimism of knaves and imbeciles. . . . They don't want to be pulled up by
any sane considerations. . . ."

For some moments he kept silence—as if in
unspeakable commination.

"Here I am with some clearness of vision—my
only gift; not very clever, with a natural bad temper, and a strong sexual bias, doing what I can
to get a broader handling of the fuel question—as
a common interest for all mankind. And I find
myself up against a lot of men, subtle men, sharp
men, obstinate men, prejudiced men, able to get
round me, able to get over me, able to blockade
me. . . . Clever men—yes, and all of them ulti-

mately damned—oh! utterly damned—fools. Coal
owners who think only of themselves, solicitors
who think backwards, politicians who think like a
game of cat's-cradle, not a gleam of generosity—
not a gleam.''

''What particularly are you working for?''
asked the doctor.

''I want to get the whole business of the world's
fuel discussed and reported upon as one affair—
so that some day it may be handled as one affair—
in the general interest.''

''The world, did you say? You meant the
empire?''

''No, the world. It is all one system now. You
can't work it in bits. I want to call in foreign
representatives from the beginning.''

''Advisory—consultative?''

''No. With powers. These things interlock
now internationally both through labour and
finance. The sooner we scrap this nonsense about
an autonomous British Empire complete in itself,
contra mundum, the better for us. A world control is fifty years overdue. Hence these
disorders.''

''Still,—it's rather a difficult proposition, as
things are.''

''Oh, Lord! don't I know it's difficult!'' cried
Sir Richmond in the tone of one who swears.
''Don't I know that perhaps it's impossible! But
it's the only way to do it. Therefore, I say, let's

try to get it done. And everybody says, 'difficult, difficult,' and nobody lifts a finger to try. And the only real difficulty is that everybody for one reason or another says that it's difficult. It's against human nature. Granted! Every decent thing is. It's socialism. Who cares? Along this line of comprehensive scientific control the world has to go or it will retrogress, it will muddle and rot. . . .''

"I agree," said Dr. Martineau.

"So I want a report to admit that distinctly. I want it to go further than that. I want to get the beginnings, the germ, of a world administration. I want to set up a permanent world commission of scientific men and economists—with powers, just as considerable powers as I can give them —they'll be feeble powers at the best—but still some sort of *say* in the whole fuel supply of the world. A say—that may grow at last to a control. A right to collect reports and receive accounts for example, to begin with. And then the right to make recommendations. . . . You see? . . . No, the international part is not the most difficult part of it. But my beastly owners and their beastly lawyers won't relinquish a scrap of what they call their freedom of action. And my labour men, because I'm a fairly big coal owner myself, sit and watch and suspect me, too stupid to grasp what I am driving at and too incompetent to get out a scheme of their own. They want a world control on scientific lines even less than the owners. They try to think that fuel production can carry an unlimited wages bill and the owners try to think that it can pay unlimited profits, and when I say; 'This business is something more than a scramble for profits and wages; it's a service and a common interest,' they stare at me——" Sir Richmond was at a loss for an image. "Like a committee in a thieves' kitchen when someone has casually mentioned the law."

"But will you ever get your Permanent Commission?"

"It can be done. If I can stick it out."

"But with the whole Committee against you!"

"The curious thing is that the whole Committee isn't against me. Every individual is. . . ."

Sir Richmond found it difficult to express. "The psychology of my Committee ought to interest you. . . . It is probably a fair sample of the way all sorts of things are going nowadays. It's curious. . . . There is not a man on that Committee who is quite comfortable within himself about the particular individual end he is there to serve. It's there I get them. They pursue their own ends bitterly and obstinately I admit, but they are bitter and obstinate because they pursue them against an internal opposition—which is on my side. They are terrified to think, if once they stopped fighting me, how far they might not have to go with me."

"A suppressed world conscience in fact. This marches very closely with my own ideas——"

"A world conscience? World conscience? I don't know. But I do know that there is this drive in nearly every member of the Committee, some drive anyhow, towards the decent thing. It is the same drive that drives me. But I am the most driven. It has turned me round. It hasn't turned them. I go East and they go West. And they don't want to be turned round. Tremendously, they don't."

"Creative undertow," said Dr. Martineau, making notes, as it were. "An increasing force in modern life. In the psychology of a new age—strengthened by education—it may play a directive part."

"They fight every little point. But, you see, because of this creative undertow—if you like to call it that—we do get along. I am leader or whipper-in, it is hard to say which, of a bolting flock. . . . I believe they will report for a permanent world commission; I believe I have got them up to that; but they will want to make it a bureau of this League of Nations, and I have the profoundest distrust of this League of Nations. It may turn out to be a sort of side-tracking arrangement for all sorts of important world issues. And they will find they have to report for some sort of control. But there again they will shy. They will report for it and then they will do their utmost to whittle it down again. They will refuse it the most reasonable powers. They will alter the composition of the Committee so as to make it innocuous.''

''How?''

''Get rid of the independent scientific men, load it up so far as Britain is concerned with muck of the colonial politician type and tame labour representatives, balance with shady new adventurer millionaires, get in still shadier stuff from abroad, let these gentry appoint their own tame experts after their own hearts,—experts who will make merely advisory reports, which will not be published. . . .''

''They want in fact to keep the old system going under the cloak of *your* Committee, reduced to a cloak and nothing more?''

''That is what it amounts to. They want to have the air of doing right—indeed they do want to have the *feel* of doing right—and still leave things just exactly what they were before. And as I suffer under the misfortune of seeing the thing rather more clearly, I have to shepherd the conscience of the whole Committee. . . . But there is a conscience there. If I can hold out myself, I can hold the Committee.''

He turned appealingly to the doctor. ''Why should I have to be the conscience of that damned Committee? Why should I do this exhausting inhuman job? . . . In their hearts these others know. . . . Only they won't know. . . . Why should it fall on me?''

"You have to go through with it," said Dr. Martineau.

"I have to go through with it, but it's a hell of utterly inglorious squabbling. They bait me. They have been fighting the same fight within themselves that they fight with me. They know exactly where I am, that I too am doing my job against internal friction. The one thing before all others that they want to do is to bring me down off my moral high horse. And I loathe the high horse. I am in a position of special moral superiority to men who are on the whole as good men as I am or better. That shows all the time. You see the sort of man I am. I've a broad streak of personal vanity. I fag easily. I'm short-tempered. I've other things, as you perceive. When I fag I become obtuse, I repeat and bore, I get viciously ill-tempered, I suffer from an intolerable sense of ill usage. Then that ass, Wagstaffe, who ought to be working with me steadily, sees his chance to be pleasantly witty. He gets a laugh round the table at my expense. Young Dent, the more intelligent of the labour men, reads me a lecture in committee manners. Old Cassidy sees *his* opening and jabs some ridiculous petty accusation at me and gets me spluttering self-defence like a fool. All my stock goes down, and as my stock goes down the chances of a good report dwindle. Young Dent grieves to see me injuring my own case. Too damned a fool to see what will happen to the report! You see if only they can convince themselves I am just a prig and an egotist and an impractical bore, they escape from a great deal more than my poor propositions. They escape from the doubt in themselves. By dismissing me they dismiss their own consciences. And then they can scamper off and be sensible little piggy-wigs and not bother any more about what is to happen to mankind in the long run. . . . Do you begin to realize the sort of fight, upside down in a dustbin, that that Committee is for me?"

"You have to go through with it," Dr. Martineau repeated.

"I have. If I can. But I warn you I have been near breaking point. And if I tumble off the high horse, if I can't keep going regularly there to ride the moral high horse, that Committee will slump into utter scoundrelism. It will turn out a long, inconsistent, botched, unreadable report that will back up all sorts of humbugging bargains and sham settlements. It will contain some half-baked scheme to pacify the miners at the expense of the general welfare. It won't even succeed in doing that. But in the general confusion old Cassidy will get away with a series of hauls that may run into millions. Which will last his time—damn him! And that is where we are. . . . Oh! I know! I know! . . . I must do this job. I don't need any telling that my life will be nothing and mean nothing unless I bring this thing through. . . .

"But the thanklessness of playing this lone hand!"

The doctor watched his friend's resentful black silhouette against the lights on the steely river, and said nothing for awhile.

"Why did I ever undertake to play it?" Sir Richmond appealed. "Why has it been put upon me? Seeing what a poor thing I am, why am I not a poor thing altogether?"

§ 8

"I think I understand that loneliness of yours," said the doctor after an interval.

"I am *intolerable* to myself."

"And I think it explains why it is that you turn to women as you do. You want help; you want reassurance. And you feel they can give it."

"I wonder if it has been quite like that," Sir Richmond reflected.

By an effort Dr. Martineau refrained from mentioning the mother complex. "You want help and reassurance as a child does," he said. "Women and women alone seem capable of giving that, of telling you that you are surely right, that notwithstanding your blunders you are right; that even when you are wrong it doesn't so much matter, you are still in spirit right. They can show their belief in you as no man can. With all their being they can do that."

"Yes, I suppose they could."

"They can. You have said already that women are necessary to make things real for you."

"Not my work," said Sir Richmond. "I admit that it might be like that, but it isn't like that. It has not worked out like that. The two drives go on side by side in me. They have no logical connexion. All I can say is that for me, with my bifid temperament, one makes a rest from the other, and is so far refreshment and a renewal of energy. But I do not find women coming into my work in any effectual way."

The doctor reflected further. "I suppose," he began and stopped short.

He heard Sir Richmond move in his chair, creaking an interrogation.

"You have never," said the doctor, "turned to the idea of God?"

Sir Richmond grunted and made no other answer for the better part of a minute.

As Dr. Martineau waited for his companion to speak, a falling star streaked the deep blue above them.

"I can't believe in a God," said Sir Richmond.

"Something after the fashion of a God," said the doctor insidiously.

"No," said Sir Richmond. "Nothing that reassures."

"But this loneliness, this craving for companionship——"

"We have all been through that," said Sir Richmond. "We have all in our time lain very still in the darkness with our souls crying out for the fellowship of God, demanding some sign, some personal response. The faintest feeling of assurance would have satisfied us."

"And there has never been a response?"

"Have *you* ever had a response?"

"Once I seemed to have a feeling of exaltation and security."

"Well?"

"Perhaps I only persuaded myself that I had. I had been reading William James on religious experiences and I was thinking very much of 'Conversion.' . . . I tried to experience Conversion. . . ."

"Yes?"

"It faded."

"It always fades," said Sir Richmond with anger in his voice. "I wonder how many people there are nowadays who have passed through this last experience of ineffectual invocation, this appeal to the fading shadow of a vanished God. In the night. In utter loneliness. 'Answer me! Speak to me!' Does he answer? In the silence you hear the little blood vessels whisper in your ears. You see a faint glow of colour on the darkness. . . ."

Dr. Martineau sat without a word.

"I can believe that over all things Righteousness rules. I can believe that. But Righteousness is not friendliness nor mercy nor comfort nor any such dear and intimate things. This cuddling up to Righteousness! It is a dream, a delusion and a phase. I've tried all that long ago. I've given it up long ago. I've grown out of it. Men do—after forty. Our souls were made in the squatting-place of the submen of ancient times. They are made out of primitive needs and they die before our bodies as those needs are satisfied. Only young people have souls, complete. The need for a personal God, feared but reassuring, is a youth's need. I no longer fear the Old Man nor want to propitiate the Old Man nor believe he matters any more. I'm a bit of an Old Man myself I discover. Yes. . . . But the other thing still remains."

"The Great Mother of the Gods," said Dr. Martineau—still clinging to his theories.

"The need of the woman," said Sir Richmond. "I want mating because it is my nature to mate. I want fellowship because I am a social animal— and I want it from another social animal. Not from any God—any inconceivable God. Who fades and disappears. No. . . .

"Perhaps that other need will fade presently. I do not know. Perhaps it lasts as long as life does. How can I tell? . . ."

He was silent for a little while. Then his voice sounded in the night, as if he spoke to himself. "But as for the God of All Things consoling and helping! Imagine it! That up there—having fellowship with me! I would as soon think of cooling my throat with the Milky Way or shaking hands with those stars."

CHAPTER THE FIFTH

IN THE LAND OF THE FORGOTTEN PEOPLES

§ 1

A GUST of confidence on the part of a person
naturally or habitually reserved will often be followed by a phase of recoil. At breakfast next
morning their overnight talk seemed to both Sir
Richmond and Dr. Martineau like something each
had dreamt about the other, a quite impossible
excess of intimacy. They discussed the weather,
which seemed to be settling down to the utmost
serenity of which the English spring is capable,
they talked of Sir Richmond's coming car and of
the possible routes before them. Sir Richmond
produced the Michelin maps which he had taken
out of the pockets of the little Charmeuse. The
Bath Road lay before them, he explained, Reading, Newbury, Hungerford, Marlborough, Silbury
Hill which overhangs Avebury. Both travellers
discovered a common excitement at the mention
of Avebury and Silbury Hill. Both took an intelligent interest in archæology. Both had been
greatly stimulated by the recent work of Elliot
Smith and Rivers upon what was then known as

99

the Heliolithic culture. It had revived their interest in Avebury and Stonehenge. The doctor moreover had been reading Hippisley Cox's *Green Roads of England*.

Neither gentleman had ever seen Avebury, but Dr. Martineau had once visited Stonehenge.

"Avebury is much the oldest," said the doctor. "They must have made Silbury Hill long before 2000 B.C. It may be five thousand years old or even more. It is the most important historical relic in the British Isles. And the most neglected."

They exchanged archæological facts. The secret places of the heart rested until the afternoon.

Then Sir Richmond saw fit to amplify his confessions in one particular.

§ 2

The doctor and his patient had discovered a need for exercise as the morning advanced. They had walked by the road to Marlow and had lunched at a riverside inn, returning after a restful hour in an arbour on the lawn of this place to tea at Maidenhead. It was as they returned that Sir Richmond took up the thread of their overnight conversation again.

"In the night," he said, "I was thinking over

the account I tried to give you of my motives. A lot of it was terribly out of drawing.''

"Facts?" asked the doctor.

"No, the facts were all right. It was the atmosphere, the proportions. . . . I don't know if I gave you the effect of something Don Juan-esque? . . ."

"Vulgar poem," said the doctor remarkably. "I discounted that."

"Vulgar!"

"Intolerable. Byron in sexual psychology is like a stink in a kitchen."

Sir Richmond perceived he had struck upon the sort of thing that used to be called a pet aversion.

"I don't want you to think that I run about after women in an habitual and systematic manner. Or that I deliberately hunt them in the interests of my work and energy. Your questions had set me theorizing about myself. And I did my best to improvise a scheme of motives yesterday. It was, I perceive, a jerry-built scheme, run up at short notice. My nocturnal reflections convinced me of that. I put reason into things that are essentially instinctive. The truth is that the wanderings of desire have no single drive. All sorts of motives come in, high and low, down to sheer vulgar imitativeness and competitiveness. What was true in it all was this, that a man with any imagination in a fatigue phase falls naturally into these complications because they are more attractive to his type and far easier and more refreshing to the mind, at the outset, than anything else.   And they do work a sort of recovery in him. They send him back to his work refreshed—so far, that is, as his work is concerned.''

"At the *outset* they are easier," said the doctor.

Sir Richmond laughed. "When one is fagged it is only the outset counts. The more tired one is the more readily one moves along the line of least resistance. . . .

"That is one footnote to what I said. So far as the motive of my work goes, I think we got something like the spirit of it. What I said about that was near the truth of things. . . .

"But there is another set of motives altogether," Sir Richmond went on with an air of having cleared the ground for his real business, "that I didn't go into at all yesterday."

He considered. "It arises out of these other affairs. Before you realize it your affections are involved. I am a man much swayed by my affections."

Mr. Martineau glanced at him. There was a note of genuine self-reproach in Sir Richmond's voice.

"I get fond of people. It is quite irrational, but I get fond of them. Which is quite a different thing from the admiration and excitement of falling in love. Almost the opposite thing. They cry or they come some mental or physical cropper and hurt themselves, or they do something distressingly little and human and suddenly I find they've *got* me. I'm distressed. I'm filled with something between pity and an impulse of responsibility. I become tender towards them. I am impelled to take care of them. I want to ease them off, to reassure them, to make them stop hurting at any cost. I don't see why it should be the weak and sickly and seamy side of people that grips me most, but it is. I don't know why it should be their failures that gives them power over me, but it is. I told you of this girl, this mistress of mine, who is ill just now. *She's* got me in that way; she's got me tremendously.''

''You did not speak of her yesterday with any morbid excess of pity,'' the doctor was constrained to remark.

''I abused her very probably. I forget exactly what I said. . . .''

The doctor offered no assistance.

''But the reason why I abuse her is perfectly plain. I abuse her because she distresses me by her misfortunes and instead of my getting anything out of her, I go out to her. But I *do* go out to her. All this time at the back of my mind I am worrying about her. She has that gift of making one feel for her. I am feeling that damned carbuncle almost as if it had been my affair instead of hers.

"That carbuncle has made me suffer—*frightfully*. . . . Why should I? It isn't mine."

He regarded the doctor earnestly. The doctor controlled a strong desire to laugh.

"I suppose the young lady——" he began.

"Oh! *she* puts in suffering all right. I've no doubt about that.

"I suppose," Sir Richmond went on, "now that I have told you so much of this affair, I may as well tell you all. It is a sort of comedy, a painful comedy, of irrelevant affections. . . ."

The doctor was prepared to be a good listener. Facts he would always listen to; it was only when people told him their theories that he would interrupt with his "Exactly."

"This young woman is a person of considerable genius. I don't know if you have seen in the illustrated papers a peculiar sort of humorous illustrations usually with a considerable amount of bite in them over the name of Martin Leeds?"

"Extremely amusing stuff."

"It is that Martin Leeds. I met her at the beginning of her career. She talks almost as well as she draws. She amused me immensely. I'm not the sort of man who waylays and besieges women and girls. I'm not the pursuing type. But I perceived that in some odd way I attracted her and I was neither wise enough nor generous enough not to let the thing develop."

"H'm," said Dr. Martineau.

"I'd never had to do with an intellectually brilliant woman before. I see now that the more imaginative force a woman has, the more likely she is to get into a state of extreme self-abandonment with any male thing upon which her imagination begins to crystallize. Before I came along she'd mixed chiefly with a lot of young artists and students, all doing nothing at all except talk about the things they were going to do. I suppose I profited by the contrast, being older and with my hands full of affairs. Perhaps something had happened that had made her recoil towards my sort of thing. I don't know. But she just let herself go at me."

"And you?"

"Let myself go too. I'd never met anything like her before. It was her wit took me. It didn't occur to me that she wasn't my contemporary and as able as I was. As able to take care of herself. All sorts of considerations that I should have shown to a sillier woman I never dreamt of showing to her. I had never met anyone so mentally brilliant before or so helpless and headlong. And so here we are on each other's hands!"

"But the child?"

"It happened to us. For four years now things have just happened to us. All the time I have been overworking, first at explosives and now at this fuel business. She too is full of her work.

Nothing stops that though everything seems to interfere with it.   And in a distraught, preoccupied way we are abominably fond of each other. 'Fond' is the word.   But we are both too busy to look after either ourselves or each other.

"She is much more incapable than I am," said Sir Richmond as if he delivered a weighed and very important judgment.

"You see very much of each other?"

"She has a flat in Chelsea and a little cottage in South Cornwall, and we sometimes snatch a few days together, away somewhere in Surrey or up the Thames or at such a place as Southend where one is lost in a crowd of inconspicuous people. When things go well—they usually go well at the start—we are glorious companions.   She is happy, she is creative, she will light up a new place with flashes of humour, with a keenness of appreciation. . . ."

"But things do not always go well?"

"Things," said Sir Richmond with the deliberation of a man who measures his words, "are apt to go wrong. . . .   At the flat there is constant trouble with the servants; they bully her.   A woman is more entangled with servants than a man.   Women in that position seem to resent the work and freedom of other women.   Her servants won't leave her in peace as they would leave a man; they make trouble for her. . . .   And when we have had a few days anywhere away, even if nothing in particular has gone wrong——''

Sir Richmond stopped short.

''When they go wrong it is generally her fault?'' the doctor sounded.

''Almost always.''

''But if they don't?'' said the psychiatrist.

''It is difficult to describe. . . . The essential incompatibility of the whole thing comes out.''

The doctor maintained his expression of intelligent interest.

''She wants to go on with her work. She is able to work anywhere. All she wants is just cardboard and ink. My mind on the other hand turns back to the Fuel Commission. . . .''

''Then any little thing makes trouble.''

''Any little thing makes trouble. And we always drift round to the same discussion; whether we ought really to go on together.''

''It is you begin that?''

''Yes, I start that. You see she is perfectly contented when I am about. She is as fond of me as I am of her.''

''Fonder perhaps.''

''I don't know. But she is—adhesive. Emotionally adhesive. All she wants to do is just to settle down when I am there and go on with her work. But then, you see, there is *my* work.''

''Exactly. . . . After all it seems to me that

your great trouble is not in yourselves but in social institutions. Which haven't yet fitted themselves to people like you two. It is the sense of
uncertainty makes her, as you say, adhesive. Nervously so. If we were indeed living in a new age
instead of the moral ruins of a shattered one——''

"We can't alter the age we live in," said Sir
Richmond a little testily.

"No. Exactly. But we *can* realize, in any particular situation, that it is not the individuals
to blame but the misfit of ideas and forms and
prejudices."

"No," said Sir Richmond, obstinately reject-
ing this pacifying suggestion; "she could adapt
herself. If she cared enough."

"But how?"

"She will not take the slightest trouble to
adjust herself to the peculiarities of our position.
. . . She could be cleverer. Other women are
cleverer. Any other woman almost would be
cleverer than she is."

"But if she was cleverer, she wouldn't be the
genius she is. She would just be any other
woman."

"Perhaps she would," said Sir Richmond
darkly and desperately. "Perhaps she would.
Perhaps it would be better if she was."

Dr. Martineau raised his eyebrows in a furtive
aside.

"But here you see that it is that in my case,

the fundamental incompatibility between one's affections and one's wider conception of duty and
work comes in. We cannot change social institutions in a year or a lifetime. We can never
change them to suit an individual case. That
would be like suspending the laws of gravitation
in order to move a piano. As things are, Martin
is no good to me, no help to me. She is a rival
to my duty. She feels that. She is hostile to my
duty. A definite antagonism has developed. She
feels and treats fuel and everything to do with
fuel as a bore. It is an attack. We quarrel on
that. It isn't as though I found it so easy to
stick to my work that I could disregard her hostility. And I can't bear to part from her. I
threaten it, I distress her excessively and then I
am overcome by sympathy for her and I go back
to her. . . . In the ordinary course of things I
should be with her now."

"If it were not for the carbuncle?"

"If it were not for the carbuncle. She does not
care for me to see her disfigured. She does not understand——" Sir Richmond was at a loss for
a phrase——"that it is not her good looks."

"She won't let you go to her?"

"It amounts to that. . . . And soon there will
be all the trouble about educating the girl. Whatever happens, she must have as good a chance as
—anyone. . . ."

"Ah! That is worrying you too!"

"Frightfully at times. If it were a boy it would be easier. It needs constant tact and dexterity to fix things up. Neither of us have any. It needs attention. . . ."

Sir Richmond mused darkly.

Dr. Martineau thought aloud. "An incompetent delightful person with Martin Leeds's sense of humour. And her powers of expression. She must be attractive to many people. She could probably do without you. If once you parted."

Sir Richmond turned on him eagerly.

"You think I ought to part from her? On her account?"

"On her account. It might pain her. But once the thing was done——"

"I want to part. I believe I ought to part."

"Well?"

"But then my affection comes in."

"That extraordinary—*tenderness* of yours?"

"I'm afraid."

"Of what?"

"Anyone might get hold of her—if I let her down. She hasn't a tithe of the ordinary cool-headed calculation of an average woman. . . . I've a duty to her genius. I've got to take care of her."

To which the doctor made no reply.

"Nevertheless the idea of parting has been very much in my mind lately."

"Letting her go free?"

"You can put it in that way if you like."

"It might not be a fatal operation for either of you."

"And yet there are moods when parting is an intolerable idea. When one is invaded by a flood of affection." . . . And old habits of association."

Dr. Martineau thought. Was that the right word,—affection? Perhaps it was.

They had come out on the towing path close by the lock and they found themselves threading their way through a little crowd of boating people and lookers-on. For a time their conversation was broken. Sir Richmond resumed it.

"But this is where we cease to be Man on his Planet and all the rest of it. This is where the idea of a definite task, fanatically followed to the exclusion of all minor considerations, breaks down. When the work is good, when we are sure we are all right, then we may carry off things with a high hand. But the work isn't always good, we aren't always sure. We blunder, we make a muddle, we are fatigued. Then the sacrificed affections come in as accusers. Then it is that we want to be reassured."

"And then it is that Miss Martin Leeds——?"

"Doesn't," Sir Richmond snapped.

Came a long pause.

"And yet——

"It is extraordinarily difficult to think of parting from Martin."

§ 3

In the evening after dinner Dr. Martineau sought, rather unsuccessfully, to go on with the analysis of Sir Richmond.

But Sir Richmond was evidently a creature of moods. Either he regretted the extent of his confidences or the slight irrational irritation that he felt at waiting for his car affected his attitude towards his companion, or Dr. Martineau's tentatives were ill-chosen. At any rate he would not rise to any conversational bait that the doctor could devise. The doctor found this the more regrettable because it seemed to him that there was much to be worked upon in this Martin Leeds affair. He was inclined to think that she and Sir Richmond were unduly obsessed by the idea that they had to stick together because of the child, because of the look of the thing and so forth, and that really each might be struggling against a very strong impulse indeed to break off the affair. It seemed evident to the doctor that they jarred upon and annoyed each other extremely. On the whole separating people appealed to the doctor's mind more strongly than bringing them together. Accordingly he framed his enquiries so as to make the revelation of a latent antipathy as easy as possible.

He made several not very well-devised beginnings. At the fifth Sir Richmond was suddenly conclusive. "It's no use," he said, "I can't fiddle about any more with my motives to-day."

An awkward silence followed. On reflection Sir Richmond seemed to realize that this sentence needed some apology. "I admit," he said, "that this expedition has already been a wonderfully good thing for me. These confessions have made me look into all sorts of things—squarely. But——

"I'm not used to talking about myself or even thinking directly about myself. What I say, I afterwards find disconcerting to recall. I want to alter it. I can feel myself wallowing into a mess of modifications and qualifications."

"Yes, but——"

"I want a rest anyhow. . . ."

There was nothing for Dr. Martineau to say to that.

The two gentlemen smoked for some time in a slightly uncomfortable silence. Dr. Martineau cleared his throat twice and lit a second cigar. They then agreed to admire the bridge and think well of Maidenhead. Sir Richmond communicated hopeful news about his car, which was to arrive the next morning before ten—he'd just ring the fellow up presently to make sure—and Dr. Martineau retired early and went rather thoughtfully to bed. The spate of Sir Richmond's confidences, it was evident, was over.

§ 4

Sir Richmond's car arrived long before ten, brought down by a young man in a state of scared alacrity—Sir Richmond had done some vigorous telephoning before turning in,—the Charmeuse set off in a repaired and chastened condition to town, and after a leisurely breakfast our two investigators into the springs of human conduct were able to resume their westward journey. They ran through scattered Twyford with its pleasant-looking inns and through the commonplace urbanities of Reading, by Newbury and Hungerford's pretty bridge and up long wooded slopes to Savernake forest, where they found the road heavy and dusty, still in its war-time state, and so down a steep hill to the wide market street which is Marlborough. They lunched in Marlborough and went on in the afternoon to Silbury Hill, that British pyramid, the largest artificial mound in Europe. They left the car by the roadside and clambered to the top and were very learned and inconclusive about the exact purpose of this vast heap of chalk and earth, this heap that men had made before the temples at Karnak were built or Babylon had a name

Then they returned to the car and ran round by a winding road into the wonder of Avebury. They found a clean little inn there kept by pleas-

ant people, and they garaged the car in the cow-
shed and took two rooms for the night that they
might the better get the atmosphere of the ancient place. Wonderful indeed it is, a vast circumvallation that was already two thousand years
old before the dawn of British history; a great
wall of earth with its ditch most strangely on its
inner and not on its outer side; and within this
enclosure gigantic survivors of the great circles
of unhewn stone that, even as late as Tudor days,
were almost complete. A whole village, a church,
a pretty manor house have been built, for the most
part, out of the ancient megaliths; the great wall
is sufficient to embrace them all with their gardens
and paddocks; four cross-roads meet at the village centre. There are drawings of Avebury before these things arose there, when it was a lonely
wonder on the plain, but for the most part the
destruction was already done before the *Mayflower*
sailed. To the southward stands the cone of Silbury Hill; its shadow creeps up and down the in-
tervening meadows as the seasons change. Around
this lonely place rise the Downs, now bare sheep
pastures, in broad undulations, with a wart-like
barrow here and there, and from it radiate, creeping up to gain and hold the crests of the hills,
the abandoned trackways of that forgotten world.
These trackways, these green roads of England,
these roads already disused when the Romans
made their highway past Silbury Hill to Bath,

can still be traced for scores of miles through the land, running to Salisbury and the English Channel, eastward to the crossing at the Straits and westward to Wales, to ferries over the Severn, and southwestward into Devon and Cornwall.

The doctor and Sir Richmond walked round the walls, surveyed the shadow cast by Silbury upon the river flats, strolled up the down to the northward to get a general view of the village, had tea and smoked round the walls again in the warm April sunset. The matter of their conversation remained prehistoric. Both were inclined to find fault with the archæological work that had been done on the place. "Clumsy treasure hunting," Sir Richmond said. "They bore into Silbury Hill and expect to find a mummified chief or something sensational of that sort, and they don't, and they report—nothing. They haven't sifted finely enough; they haven't thought subtly enough. These walls of earth ought to tell what these people ate, what clothes they wore, what woods they used. Was this a sheep land then as it is now, or a cattle land? Were these hills covered by forests? I don't know. These archæologists don't know. Or if they do they haven't told me,—which is just as bad. I don't believe they know.

"What trade came here along these tracks? So far as I know, they had no beasts of burthen. But suppose one day someone were to find a potsherd here from early Knossos, or a fragment of glass from Pepi's Egypt.''

The place had stirred up his imagination. He wrestled with his ignorance as if he thought that by talking he might presently worry out some picture of this forgotten world, without metals, without beasts of burthen, without letters, without any sculpture that has left a trace, and yet with a sense of astronomical fact clear enough to raise the great gnomon of Silbury, and with a social system complex enough to give the large and orderly community to which the size of Avebury witnesses and the traffic to which the green roads testify.

The doctor had not realized before the boldness and liveliness of his companion's mind. Sir Richmond insisted that the climate must have been moister and milder in those days; he covered all the downlands with woods, as Savernake was still covered; beneath the trees he restored a thicker, richer soil. These people must have done an enormous lot with wood. This use of stones here was a freak. It was the very strangeness of stones here that had made them into sacred things. One thought too much of the stones of the Stone Age. Who would carve these lumps of quartzite when one could carve good oak? Or beech—a most carvable wood. Especially when one's sharpest chisel was a flint. "It's wood we ought to look for,"

said Sir Richmond. "Wood and fibre." He declared that these people had their tools of wood,
their homes of wood, their gods and perhaps their
records of wood. "A peat bog here, even a few
feet of clay, might have pickled some precious
memoranda. . . . No such luck. . . ." Now in
Glastonbury marshes one found the life of the
early iron age—half way to our own times—quite
beautifully pickled.

Though they wrestled mightily with the problem, neither Sir Richmond nor the doctor could
throw a gleam of light upon the riddle why the
ditch was inside and not outside the great wall.

"And what was our Mind like in those days?"
said Sir Richmond. "That, I suppose, is what interests you. A vivid childish mind, I guess, with
not a suspicion as yet that it was Man ruling his
Planet or anything of that sort."

The doctor pursed his lips. "None," he delivered judicially. "If one were able to recall
one's childhood—at the age of about twelve or
thirteen—when the artistic impulse so often goes
into abeyance and one begins to think in a troubled, monstrous way about God and Hell, one
might get something like the mind of this place."

"Thirteen. You put them at that—already?
. . . These people, you think, were religious?"

"Intensely. In that personal way that gives
death a nightmare terror. And as for the fading
of the artistic impulse, they've left not a trace of

the paintings and drawings and scratchings of the Old Stone people who came before them.''

''Adults with the minds of thirteen-year-old children. Thirteen-year-old children with the strength of adults—and no one to slap them or tell them not to. . . . After all, they probably only thought of death now and then. And they never thought of fuel. They supposed there was no end to that. So they used up their woods and kept goats to nibble and kill the new undergrowth. . . . *Did* these people have goats?''

''I don't know,'' said the doctor. ''So little is known.''

''Very like children they must have been. The same unending days. They must have thought that the world went on for ever—just as they knew it—like my damned Committee does. . . . With their fuel wasting away and the climate changing imperceptibly, century by century. . . . Kings and important men followed one another here for centuries and centuries. . . . They had lost their past and had no idea of any future. . . . They had forgotten how they came into the land . . . When I was a child I believed that my father's garden had been there for ever. . . .

''This is very like trying to remember some game one played when one was a child. It is like coming on something that one built up with bricks and stones in some forgotten part of the garden. . . .''

"The life we lived here," said the doctor, "has left its traces in traditions, in mental predispositions, in still unanalyzed fundamental ideas."

"Archæology is very like remembering," said Sir Richmond. "Presently we shall remember a lot more about all this. We shall remember what it was like to live in this place, and the long journey hither, age by age out of the south. We shall remember the sacrifices we made and the crazy reasons why we made them. We sowed our corn in blood here. We had strange fancies about the stars. Those we brought with us out of the south where the stars are brighter. And what like were those wooden gods of ours? I don't remember. . . . But I could easily persuade myself that I had been here before."

They stood on the crest of the ancient wall and the setting sun cast long shadows of them athwart a field of springing wheat.

"Perhaps we shall come here again," the doctor carried on Sir Richmond's fancy; "after another four thousand years or so, with different names and fuller minds. And then I suppose that this ditch won't be the riddle it is now."

"Life didn't seem so complicated then," Sir Richmond mused. "Our muddles were unconscious. We drifted from mood to mood and forgot. There was more sunshine then, more laughter perhaps, and blacker despair. Despair like the despair of children that can weep itself to sleep.

. . . It's over. . . . Was it battle and massacre that ended that long afternoon here? Or did the woods catch fire some exceptionally dry summer, leaving black hills and famine? Or did strange men bring a sickness—measles, perhaps, or the black death? Or was it cattle pest? Or did we just waste our woods and dwindle away before the new peoples that came into the land across the southern sea? I can't remember. . . ."

Sir Richmond turned about. "I would like to dig up the bottom of this ditch here foot by foot—and dry the stuff and sift it—very carefully. . . . Then I might begin to remember things."

§ 5

In the evening, after a pleasant supper, they took a turn about the walls with the moon sinking over beyond Silbury, and then went in and sat by lamplight before a brightly fussy wood fire and smoked. There were long intervals of friendly silence.

"I don't in the least want to go on talking about myself," said Sir Richmond abruptly.

"Let it rest then," said the doctor generously.

"To-day, among these ancient memories, has taken me out of myself wonderfully. I can't tell you how good Avebury has been for me. This afternoon half my consciousness has seemed to

be a tattooed creature wearing a knife of
stone. . . ."

"The healing touch of history."

"And for the first time my damned Committee
has mattered scarcely a rap."

Sir Richmond stretched himself in his chair and
blinked cheerfully at his cigar smoke.

"Nevertheless," he said, "this confessional
business of yours has been an excellent exercise.
It has enabled me to get outside myself, to look at
myself as a Case. Now I can even see myself as a
remote Case. That I needn't bother about further. . . . So far as that goes, I think we have
done all that there is to be done."

"I shouldn't say that—quite—yet," said the
doctor.

"I don't think I'm a subject for real psychoanalysis at all. I'm not an overlaid sort of person. When I spread myself out there is not much
indication of a suppressed wish or of anything
masked or buried of that sort. What you get is
a quite open and recognized discord of two sets
of motives."

The doctor considered. "Yes, I think that is
true. Your *libido* is, I should say, exceptionally
free. Generally you are doing what you want to
do—overdoing, in fact, what you want to do—
and getting simply tired."

"Which is the theory I started with. I am a
case of fatigue under irritating circumstances

with very little mental complication or conceal-
ment.''

"Yes," said the doctor. "I agree. You are
not a case for psychoanalysis, strictly speaking,
at all. You are in open conflict with yourself
upon moral and social issues. Practically open.
Your problems are problems of conscious conduct.''

"As I said."

"Of what renunciations you have consciously
to make.''

Sir Richmond did not answer that. . . .

"This pilgrimage of ours," he said, presently,
"has made for magnanimity. This day particularly has been a good day. When we stood on this
old wall here in the sunset I seemed to be standing
outside myself in an immense still sphere of past
and future. I stood with my feet upon the Stone
Age and saw myself four thousand years away,
and all my distresses as very little incidents in
that perspective. Away there in London the case
is altogether different; after three hours or so
of the Committee one concentrates into one little
inflamed moment of personality. There is no past
any longer, there is no future, there is only the
rankling dispute. For all those three hours, perhaps, I have been thinking of just what I had to
say, just how I had to say it, just how I looked
while I said it, just how much I was making myself understood, how I might be misunderstood,

how I might be misrepresented, challenged, denied. One draws in more and more as one is used up. At last one is reduced to a little, raw, bleeding, desperately fighting, pin-point of *self*. . . . One goes back to one's home unable to recover. Fighting it over again. All night sometimes. . . . I get up and walk about the room and curse. . . . Martineau, how is one to get the Avebury frame of mind to Westminster?''

''When Westminster is as dead as Avebury,'' said the doctor, unhelpfully. He added after some seconds, ''Milton knew of these troubles. 'Not without dust and heat,' he wrote—a great phrase.''

''But the dust chokes me,'' said Sir Richmond.

He took up a copy of *The Green Roads of England* that lay beside him on the table. But he did not open it. He held it in his hand and said the thing he had had in mind to say all that evening. ''I do not think that I shall stir up my motives any more for a time. Better to go on into the west country cooling my poor old brain in these wide shadows of the past.''

''I can prescribe nothing better,'' said Dr. Martineau. ''Incidentally, we may be able to throw a little more light on one or two of your minor entanglements.''

''I don't want to think of them,'' said Sir Richmond. ''Let me get right away from everything. Until my skin has grown again.''

CHAPTER THE SIXTH

THE ENCOUNTER AT STONEHENGE

§ 1

Next day in the early afternoon after a farewell walk over the downs round Avebury they went by way of Devizes and Netheravon and Amesbury to Stonehenge.

Dr. Martineau had seen this ancient monument before, but now, with Avebury fresh in his mind, he found it a poorer thing than he had remembered it to be. Sir Richmond was frankly disappointed. After the real greatness and mystery of the older place, it seemed a poor little heap of stones; it did not even dominate the landscape; it was some way from the crest of the swelling down on which it stood and it was further dwarfed by the colossal air-ship hangars and clustering offices of the air station that the great war had called into existence upon the slopes to the south-west. "It looks," Sir Richmond said, "as though some old giantess had left a discarded set of teeth on the hillside." Far more impressive than Stonehenge itself were the barrows that capped the neighbouring crests.

The sacred stones were fenced about, and our visitors had to pay for admission at a little kiosk by the gate. At the side of the road stood a travel-stained middle-class automobile, with a miscellany of dusty luggage, rugs and luncheon things therein—a family automobile with father no doubt at the wheel. Sir Richmond left his own trim coupé at its tail.

They were impeded at the entrance by a difference of opinion between the keeper of the turnstile and a small but resolute boy of perhaps five or six who proposed to leave the enclosure. The custodian thought that it would be better if his nurse or his mother came out with him.

"She keeps on looking at it," said the small boy. "It isunt anything. I want to go and clean the car."

"You won't see Stonehenge every day, young man," said the custodian, a little piqued.

"It's only an old beach," said the small boy, with extreme conviction. "It's rocks like the seaside. And there isunt no sea."

The man at the turnstile mutely consulted the doctor.

"I don't see that he can get into any harm here," the doctor advised, and the small boy was released from archæology.

He strolled to the family automobile, produced an *en-tout-cas* pocket-handkerchief and set himself to polish the lamps with great assiduity. The two gentlemen lingered at the turnstile for a moment or so to watch his proceedings. "Modern child," said Sir Richmond. "Old stones are just old stones to him. But motor cars are gods."

"You can hardly expect him to understand— at his age," said the custodian, jealous for the honor of Stonehenge. . . .

"Reminds me of Martir's little girl," said Sir Richmond, as he and Dr. Martineau went on towards the circle. "When she encountered her first dragon-fly she was greatly delighted. 'Oh, dee' lill' a'eplane,' she said."

As they approached the grey old stones they became aware of a certain agitation among them. A voice, an authoritative bass voice, was audible, crying, "Anthony!" A nurse appeared remotely going in the direction of the aeroplane sheds, and her cry of "Master Anthony" came faintly on the breeze. An extremely pretty young woman of five or six and twenty became visible standing on one of the great prostrate stones in the centre of the place. She was a black-haired, sun-burnt individual and she stood with her arms akimbo, quite frankly amused at the disappearance of Master Anthony, and offering no sort of help for his recovery. On the greensward before her stood the paterfamilias of the family automobile, and he was making a trumpet with his hands in order to repeat the name of Anthony with greater effect. A short lady in grey emerged from among the encircling megaliths, and one or two other feminine personalities produced effects of movement rather than of individuality as they flitted among the stones. "Well," said the lady in grey, with that rising intonation of humorous conclusion which is so distinctively American, "those Druids have *got* him."

"He's hiding," said the automobilist, in a voice that promised chastisement to a hidden hearer. "That's what he's doing. He ought not to play tricks like this. A great boy who is almost six."

"If you are looking for a small, resolute boy of six," said Sir Richmond, addressing himself to the lady on the rock rather than to the angry parent below, "he's perfectly safe and happy. The Druids haven't got him. Indeed, they've failed altogether to get him. 'Stonehenge,' he says, 'is no good.' So he's gone back to clean the lamps of your car."

"Aa-oo. So *that's* it!" said Papa. "Winnie, go and tell Price he's gone back to the car. . . . They oughtn't to have let him out of the enclosure. . . .

The excitement about Master Anthony collapsed. The rest of the people in the circles crystallized out into the central space as two apparent sisters and an apparent aunt and the nurse, who was packed off at once to supervise the lamp cleaning. The head of the family found some difficulty, it would seem, in readjusting his mind to the comparative innocence of Anthony, and Sir Richmond and the young lady on the rock sought as if by common impulse to establish a general conversation. There were faint traces of excitement in her manner, as though there had been some controversial passage between herself and the family gentleman.

"We were discussing the age of this old place," she said, smiling in the frankest and friendliest way. "How old do *you* think it is?"

The father of Anthony intervened, also with a shadow of controversy in his manner. "I was explaining to the young lady that it dates from the early bronze age. Before chronology existed. . . . But she insists on dates."

"Nothing of bronze has ever been found here," said Sir Richmond.

"Well, when was this early bronze age, anyhow?" said the young lady.

Sir Richmond sought a recognizable datum. "Bronze got to Britain somewhere between the times of Moses and Solomon."

"Ah!" said the young lady, as who should say, 'This man at least talks sense.'

"But these stones are all shaped," said the father of the family. "It is difficult to see how that could have been done without something harder than stone."

"I don't *see* the place," said the young lady on the stone. "I can't imagine how they did it up— not one bit."

"Did it up!" exclaimed the father of the family in the tone of one accustomed to find a gentle sport in the intellectual frailties of his womenkind.

"It's just the bones of a place. They hung things round it. They draped it."

"But what things?" asked Sir Richmond.

"Oh! they had things all right. Skins perhaps. Mats of rushes. Bast cloth. Fibre of all sorts. Wadded stuff."

"Stonehenge draped! It's really a delightful idea;" said the father of the family, enjoying it.

"It's quite a possible one," said Sir Richmond.

"Or they may have used wicker," the young lady went on, undismayed. She seemed to concede a point. "Wicker *is* likelier."

"But surely," said the father of the family, with the expostulatory voice and gesture of one who would recall erring wits to sanity, "it is far more impressive standing out bare and noble as it does. In lonely splendour."

"But all this country may have been wooded then," said Sir Richmond. "In which case it wouldn't have stood out. It doesn't stand out so very much even now."

"You came to it through a grove," said the young lady, eagerly picking up the idea.

"Probably beech," said Sir Richmond.

"Which may have pointed to the midsummer sunrise," said Dr. Martineau, unheeded.

"These are *novel* ideas," said the father of the family in the reproving tone of one who never allows a novel idea inside *his* doors if he can prevent it.

"Well," said the young lady, "I guess there was some sort of show here anyhow. And no human being ever had a show yet without trying to shut people out of it in order to make them come in. I guess this was covered in all right. A dark hunched old place in a wood. Beech stems, smooth, like pillars. And they came to it at night, in procession, beating drums, and scared half out of their wits. They came in *there* and went round the inner circle with their torches. And so they were shown. The torches were put out and the priests did their mysteries. Until dawn broke. That's how they worked it."

"But even you can't tell what the show was, V.V." said the lady in grey, who was standing now at Dr. Martineau's elbow.

"Something horrid," said Anthony's younger sister to her elder in a stage whisper.

"*Bluggy,*" agreed Anthony's elder sister to the younger, in a noiseless voice that certainly did not reach father. "*Squeals! . . .*"

This young lady who was addressed as "V.V." was perhaps one or two and twenty, Dr. Martineau thought,—he was not very good at feminine ages.   She had a clear sun-browned complexion, with dark hair and smiling lips.   Her features were finely modelled, with just that added touch of breadth in the brow and softness in the cheek bones, that faint flavour of the Amerindian, one sees at times in American women.   Her voice was a very soft and pleasing voice, and she spoke persuasively and not assertively as so many American women do.   Her determination to make the dry bones of Stonehenge live shamed the doctor's disappointment with the place.   And when she had spoken, Dr. Martineau noted that she looked at Sir Richmond as if she expected him at least to confirm her vision.   Sir Richmond was evidently prepared to confirm it.

With a queer little twinge of infringed proprietorship, the doctor saw Sir Richmond step up on the prostrate megalith and stand beside her, the better to appreciate her point of view.   He smiled down at her.   "Now why do you think they came in *there?*" he asked.

The young lady was not very clear about her directions.   She did not know of the roadway running to the Avon river, nor of the alleged race course to the north, nor had she ever heard that the stones were supposed to be of two different periods and that some of them might possibly have been brought from a very great distance.

§ 2

Neither Dr. Martineau nor the father of the
family found the imaginative reconstruction of
the Stonehenge rituals quite so exciting as the two
principals.   The father of the family endured
some further particulars with manifest impatience, no longer able, now that Sir Richmond was
encouraging the girl, to keep her in check with
the slightly derisive smile proper to her sex.   Then
he proclaimed in a fine loud tenor, "All this is
very imaginative, I'm afraid."   And to his family, "Time we were pressing on.   Turps, we must
go-o.   Come, Phœbe!"

As he led his little flock towards the exit his
voice came floating back.   "Talking wanton nonsense. . . .   Any professional archæologist would
laugh, simply laugh. . . ."

He passed out of the world.

With a faint intimation of dismay Dr. Martineau realized that the two talkative ladies were not
to be removed in the family automobile with the
rest of the party.   Sir Richmond and the younger
lady went on very cheerfully to the population,
agriculture, housing and general scenery of the
surrounding Downland during the later Stone
Age.   The shorter, less attractive lady, whose ac-
cent was distinctly American, came now and stood
at the doctor's elbow.   She seemed moved to play
the part of chorus to the two upon the stone.

"When V.V. gets going," she remarked, "she makes things come alive."

Dr. Martineau hated to be addressed suddenly by strange ladies. He started, and his face. assumed the distressed politeness of the moon at its full. "Your friend," he said, "interested in archæology?"

"Interested!" said the stouter lady. "Why! She's a fiend at it. Ever since we came on Carnac."

"You've visited Carnac?"

"That's where the bug bit her," said the stout lady with a note of querulous humour. "Directly V.V. set eyes on Carnac, she just turned against all her up-bringing. 'Why wasn't I told of this before?' she said. 'What's Notre Dame to this? This is where we came from. This is the real starting point of the *Mayflower*. Belinda,' she said, 'we've got to see all we can of this sort of thing before we go back to America. They've been keeping this from us.' And that's why we're here right now instead of being shopping in Paris or London like decent American women."

The younger lady looked down on her companion with something of the calm expert attention that a plumber gives to a tap that is misbehaving, and like a plumber refrained from precipitate action. She stood with the backs of her hands resting on her hips.

"Well," she said slowly, giving most of the re-

mark to Sir Richmond and the rest to the doctor.
"It *is* nearer the beginnings of things than London or Paris."

"And nearer to us," said Sir Richmond.

"I call that—just paradoxical," said the shorter lady, who appeared to be called Belinda.

"Not paradoxical," Dr. Martineau contradicted gently. "Life is always beginning again. And this is a time of fresh beginnings."

"Now that's after V.V.'s own heart," cried the stout lady in grey. "She'll agree to all that. She's been saying it right across Europe. Rome, Paris, London; they're simply just done. They don't signify any more. They've got to be cleared away."

"You let me tell my own opinions, Belinda," said the young lady who was called V.V. "I said that if people went on building with fluted pillars and Corinthian capitals for two thousand years, it was time they were cleared up and taken away."

"Corinthian capitals?" Sir Richmond considered it and laughed cheerfully. "I suppose Europe does rather overdo that sort of thing."

"The way she went on about the Victor Emmanuele Monument!" said the lady who answered to the name of Belinda. "It gave me cold shivers to think that those Italian officers might understand English."

The lady who was called V.V. smiled as if she smiled at herself, and explained herself to Sir

Richmond. "When one is travelling about, one gets to think of history and politics in terms of architecture. I do anyhow. And those columns with Corinthian capitals have got to be a sort of symbol for me for everything in Europe that I don't want and have no sort of use for. It isn't a bad sort of capital in its way, florid and pretty, but not a patch on the Doric;—and that a whole continent should come up to it and stick at it and never get past it! . . ."

"It's the classical tradition."

"It puzzles me."

"It's the Roman Empire. That Corinthian column is a weed spread by the Romans all over western Europe."

"And it smothers the history of Europe. You can't see Europe because of it. Europe is obsessed by Rome. Everywhere Marble Arches and *Arcs de Triomphe*. You never get away from it. It is like some old gentleman who has lost his way in a speech and keeps on repeating the same thing. And can't sit down. 'The empire, gentlemen— Empire. Empire.' Rome itself is perfectly frightful. It stares at you with its great round stupid arches as though it couldn't imagine that you could possibly want anything else for ever. Saint Peter's and that frightful Monument are just the same stuff as the Baths of Caracalla and the palaces of the Cæsars. Just the same. They will make just the same sort of ruins. It goes on and goes on.''

"*Ave Roma Immortalis*,'' said Dr. Martineau.

"This Roman empire seems to be Europe's first and last idea. A fixed idea. And such a poor idea! . . . America never came out of that. It's no good telling me that it did. It escaped from it. . . . So I said to Belinda here, 'Let's burrow, if we can, under all this marble and find out what sort of people we were before this Roman empire and its acanthus weeds got hold of us.' ''

"I seem to remember at Washington, something faintly Corinthian, something called the Capitol,'' Sir Richmond reflected. "And other buildings. A Treasury.''

"That's different,'' said the young lady, so conclusively that it seemed to leave nothing more to be said on that score.

"A last twinge of Europeanism,'' she vouchsafed. "We were young in those days.''

"You are well beneath the marble here.''

She assented cheerfully.

"A thousand years before it.''

"Happy place! Happy people!''

"But even this place isn't the beginning of things here. Carnac was older than this. And older still is Avebury. Have you heard in America of Avebury? It may have predated this place, they think, by another thousand years.''

"Avebury?" said the lady who was called Belinda.

"But what is this Avebury?" asked V.V. "I've never heard of the place."

"I thought it was a lord," said Belinda.

Sir Richmond, with occasional appeals to Dr. Martineau, embarked upon an account of the glory and wonder of Avebury. Possibly he exaggerated Avebury. . . .

It was Dr. Martineau who presently brought this disquisition upon Avebury to a stop by a very remarkable gesture. He looked at his watch. He drew it out ostentatiously, a thick, respectable gold watch, for the doctor was not the sort of man to wear his watch upon his wrist. He clicked it open and looked at it. Thereby he would have proclaimed his belief this encounter was an entirely unnecessary interruption of his healing duologue with Sir Richmond, which must now be resumed.

But this action had scarcely the effect he had intended it to have. It set the young lady who was called Belinda asking about ways and means of getting to Salisbury; it brought to light the distressing fact that V.V. had the beginnings of a chafed heel. Once he had set things going they moved much too quickly for the doctor to deflect their course. He found himself called upon to make personal sacrifices to facilitate the painless transport of the two ladies to Salisbury, where

their luggage awaited them at the *Old George*
Hotel. In some way too elusive to trace, it became evident that he and Sir Richmond were to
stay at this same *Old George* Hotel. The luggage
was to be shifted to the top of the coupé, the
young lady called V.V. was to share the interior
of the car with Sir Richmond, while the lady
named Belinda, for whom Dr. Martineau was already developing a very strong dislike, was to be
thrust into an extreme proximity with him and
the balance of the luggage in the dicky seat
behind.

Sir Richmond had never met with a young
woman with a genuine historical imagination before, and he was evidently very greatly excited
and resolved to get the utmost that there was to
be got out of this encounter.

§ 3

Sir Richmond displayed a complete disregard
of the sufferings of Dr. Martineau, shamefully
compressed behind him. Of these he was to hear
later. He ran his overcrowded little car, overcrowded so far as the dicky went, over the crest
of the Down and down into Amesbury and on to
Salisbury, stopping to alight and stretch the legs
of the party when they came in sight of Old
Sarum.

"Certainly they can do with a little stretching," said Dr. Martineau grimly.

This charming young woman had seized upon the imagination of Sir Richmond to the temporary exclusion of all other considerations. The long Downland gradients, quivering very slightly with the vibration of the road, came swiftly and easily to meet and pass the throbbing little car as he sat beside her and talked to her. He fell into that expository manner which comes so easily to the native entertaining the visitor from abroad.

"In England, it seems to me there are four main phases of history. Four. Avebury, which I would love to take you to see to-morrow. Stonehenge. Old Sarum, which we shall see in a moment as a great grassy mound on our right as we come over one of these crests. Each of them represents about a thousand years. Old Sarum was Keltic; it saw the Romans and the Saxons through, and for a time it was a Norman city. Now it is pasture for sheep. Latest as yet is Salisbury,—English, real English. It may last a few centuries still. It is little more than seven hundred years old. But when I think of those great hangars back there by Stonehenge, I feel that the next phase is already beginning. Of a world one will fly to the ends of, in a week or so. Our world still. Our people, your people and mine, who are going to take wing so soon now, were made in all these places. We are visiting the old homes. I am glad I came back to it just when you were doing the same thing.''

"I'm lucky to have found a sympathetic fellow traveller," she said; "with a car."

"You're the first American I've ever met whose interest in history didn't seem——'' He sought for an inoffensive word.

"Silly? Oh! I admit it. It's true of a lot of us. Most of us. We come over to Europe as if it hadn't anything to do with us except to supply us with old pictures and curios generally. We come sight-seeing. It's romantic. It's picturesque. We stare at the natives—like visitors at a Zoo. We don't realize that we belong. . . . I know our style. . . . But we aren't all like that. Some of us are learning a bit better than that. We have one or two teachers over there to lighten our darkness. There's Professor Breasted for instance. He comes sometimes to my father's house. And there's John Harvey Robinson and Professor Hutton Webster. They've been trying to restore our memory."

"I've never heard of any of them," said Sir Richmond.

"You hear so little of America over here. It's quite a large country and all sorts of interesting things happen there nowadays. And we are waking up to history. Quite fast. We shan't always be the most ignorant people in the world. We are beginning to realize that quite a lot of things happened between Adam and the *Mayflower* that we ought to be told about. I allow it's a recent revival. The United States has been like one of those men you read about in the papers who go away from home and turn up in some distant place with their memories gone. They've forgotten what their names were or where they lived or what they did for a living; they've forgotten everything that matters. Often they have to begin again and settle down for a long time before their memories come back. That's how it has been with us. Our memory is just coming back to us.''

"And what do you find you are?''

"Europeans. Who came away from kings and churches—and Corinthian capitals.''

"You feel all this country belongs to you?''

"As much as it does to you.''

Sir Richmond smiled radiantly at her. "But if I say that America belongs to me as much as it does to you?''

"We are one people,'' she said.

"We?''

"Europe. These parts of Europe anyhow. And ourselves.''

"You are the most civilized person I've met for weeks and weeks.''

"Well, you are the first civilized person I've

met in Europe for a long time. If I understand you.''

"There are multitudes of reasonable, civilized people in Europe.''

"I've heard or seen very little of them.''

"They're scattered, I admit.''

"And hard to find.''

"So ours is a lucky meeting. I've wanted a serious talk to an American for some time. I want to know very badly what you think you are up to with the world,—our world.''

"I'm equally anxious to know what England thinks she is doing. Her ways recently have been a little difficult to understand. On any hypothesis—that is honourable to her.''

"H'm,'' said Sir Richmond.

"I assure you we don't like it. This Irish business. We feel a sort of ownership in England. It's like finding your dearest aunt torturing the cat.''

"We must talk of that,'' said Sir Richmond.

"I wish you would.''

"It is a cat and a dog—and they have been very naughty animals. And poor Aunt Britannia almost deliberately lost her temper. But I admit she hits about in a very nasty fashion.''

"And favours the dog?''

"She does.''

"I want to know all you admit.''

"You shall. And incidentally my friend and I may have the pleasure of showing you Salisbury and Avebury. If you are free?"

"We're travelling together, just we two. We're wandering about the south of England on our way to Falmouth. Where I join a father in a few days' time, and I go on with him to Paris. And if you and your friend are coming to the *Old George*——?"

"We are," said Sir Richmond.

"I see no great scandal in talking right on to bedtime. And seeing Avebury to-morrow. Why not? Perhaps if we did as the Germans do and gave our names now, it might mitigate something of the extreme informality of our behaviour."

"My name is Hardy. I've been a munition manufacturer. I was slightly wounded by a stray shell near Arras while I was inspecting some plant I had set up, and also I was hit by a stray knighthood. So my name is now Sir Richmond Hardy. My friend is a very distinguished Harley Street physician. Chiefly nervous and mental cases. His name is Dr. Martineau. He is quite as civilized as I am. He is also a philosophical writer. He is really a very wise and learned man indeed. He is full of ideas. He's stimulated me tremendously. You must talk to him."

Sir Richmond glanced over his shoulder at the subject of these commendations. Through the oval window glared an expression of malignity that made no impression whatever on his preoccupied mind.

"My name," said the young lady, "is Grammont. The war whirled me over to Europe on Red Cross work and since the peace I've been settling up things and travelling about Europe. My father is rather a big business man in New York."

"The oil Grammont?"

"He *is* rather deep in oil, I believe. He is coming over to Europe because he does not like the way your people are behaving in Mesopotamia. He is on his way to Paris now. Paris it seems is where everything is to be settled against you. Belinda is a sort of companion I have acquired for the purposes of independent travel. She was Red Cross too. I must have somebody and I cannot bear a maid. Her name is Belinda Seyffert. From Philadelphia originally. You have that? Seyffert, Grammont?"

"And Hardy?"

"Sir Richmond and Dr. Martineau."

"And—Ah!—That great green bank there just coming into sight must be Old Sarum. The little ancient city that faded away when Salisbury lifted its spire into the world. We will stop here for a little while. . . ."

Then it was that Dr. Martineau was grim about the stretching of his legs.

§ 4

The sudden prospect which now opened out before Sir Richmond of talking about history and suchlike topics with a charming companion for perhaps two whole days instead of going on with this tiresome, shamefaced, egotistical business of self-examination was so attractive to him that it took immediate possession of his mind, to the entire exclusion and disregard of Dr. Martineau's possible objections to any such modification of their original programme. When they arrived in Salisbury, the doctor did make some slight effort to suggest a different hotel from that in which the two ladies had engaged their rooms, but on the spur of the moment and in their presence he could produce no sufficient reason for refusing the accommodation the *Old George* had ready for him. He was reduced to a vague: "We don't want to inflict ourselves——" He could not get Sir Richmond aside for any adequate expression of his feelings about Miss Seyffert, before the four of them were seated together at tea amidst the mediæval modernity of the *Old George* smoking-room. And only then did he begin to realize the depth and extent of the engagements to which Sir Richmond had committed himself.

"I was suggesting that we run back to Avebury to-morrow," said Sir Richmond. "These ladies were nearly missing it."

The thing took the doctor's breath away. For the moment he could say nothing. He stared over his tea-cup dour-faced.

An objection formulated itself very slowly. "But that dicky," he whispered.

His whisper went unnoted. Sir Richmond was talking of the completeness of Salisbury. From the very beginning it had been a cathedral city; it was essentially and purely that. The church at its best, in the full tide of its mediæval ascendancy, had called it into being. He was making some extremely loose and inaccurate generalizations about the buildings and ruins each age had left for posterity, and Miss Grammont was countering with equally unsatisfactory qualifications. "Our age will leave the ruins of hotels," said Sir Richmond. "Railway arches and hotels."

"Baths and aqueducts," Miss Grammont compared. "Rome of the Empire comes nearest to it. . . ."

As soon as tea was over, Dr. Martineau realized, they meant to walk round and about Salisbury. He foresaw that walk with the utmost clearness. In front and keeping just a little beyond the range of his intervention, Sir Richmond would go with Miss Grammont; he himself and Miss Seyffert would bring up the rear. "If I do," he muttered, "I'll be damned!" an unusually strong expression for him.

"You said——?" asked Miss Seyffert.

"That I have some writing to do—before the post goes," said the doctor brightly.

"Oh! *come* and see the cathedral!" cried Sir Richmond with ill-concealed dismay. He was, if one may put it in such a fashion, *not* looking at Miss Seyffert in the directest fashion when he said this.

"I'm afraid," said the doctor mulishly. "Impossible."

(With the unspoken addition of, *"You* try her for a bit.")

Miss Grammont stood up. Everybody stood up. "We can go first to look for shops," she said. "There's those things you want to buy, Belinda; a fountain pen and the little books. We can all go together as far as that. And while you are shopping, if you wouldn't mind getting one or two things for me. . . ."

It became clear to Dr. Martineau that Sir Richmond was to be let off Belinda. It seemed abominably unjust. And it was also clear to him that he must keep closely to his own room or he might find Miss Seyffert drifting back alone to the hotel and eager to resume with him. . . .

Well, a quiet time in his room would not be disagreeable. He could think over his notes. . . .

But in reality he thought over nothing but the little speeches he would presently make to Sir Richmond about the unwarrantable, the absolutely unwarrantable, alterations that were being made without his consent in their common programme. . . .

For a long time Sir Richmond had met no one so interesting and amusing as this frank-minded young woman from America. "Young woman" was how he thought of her; she didn't correspond to anything so prim and restrained and extensively reserved and withheld as a "young lady"; and though he judged her no older than five and twenty, the word "girl" with its associations of virginal ignorances, invisible purdah, and trite ideas newly discovered, seemed even less appropriate for her than the word "boy." She had an air of having in some obscure way graduated in life, as if so far she had lived each several year of her existence in a distinctive and conclusive manner with the utmost mental profit and no particular tarnish or injury. He could talk with her as if he talked with a man like himself—but with a zest no man could give him.

It was evident that the good things she had said at first came as the natural expression of a broad stream of alert thought; they were no mere display specimens from one of those jackdaw collections of bright things so many clever women waste their wits in accumulating. She was not talking for effect at all, she was talking because she was tremendously interested in her discovery of the spectacle of history, and delighted to find another person as possessed as she was.

Belinda having been conducted to her shops, the two made their way through the bright evening sunlight to the compact gracefulness of the cathedral. A glimpse through a wrought-iron gate of a delightful garden of spring flowers, alyssum, aubrietia, snow-upon-the-mountains, daffodils, narcissus and the like, held them for a time, and then they came out upon the level, grassy space, surrounded by little ripe old houses, on which the cathedral stands. They stood for some moments surveying it.

"It's a perfect little lady of a cathedral," said Sir Richmond. "But why, I wonder, did we build it?"

"Your memory ought to be better than mine," she said, with her half-closed eyes blinking up at the sunlit spire sharp against the blue. "I've been away for so long—over there—that I forget altogether. Why *did* we build it?"

She had fallen in quite early with this freak of speaking and thinking as if he and she were all mankind. It was as if her mind had been prepared for it by her own eager exploration in Europe. "My friend, the philosopher," he had said, "will not have it that we are really the individuals we think we are. You must talk to him—he is a very curious and subtle thinker. We are just thoughts in the Mind of the Race, he says, passing thoughts. We are—what does he call it? —Man on his Planet, taking control of life."

"Man and woman," she had amended.

But just as man on his planet taking control of life had failed altogether to remember why the ditch at Avebury was on the inside instead of the outside of the vallum, so now Miss Grammont and Sir Richmond found very great difficulty in recalling why they had built Salisbury Cathedral.

"We built temples by habit and tradition," said Sir Richmond. "But the impulse was losing its force."

She looked up at the spire and then at him with a faintly quizzical expression.

But he had his reply ready.

"We were beginning to feel our power over matter. We were already very clever engineers. What interested us here wasn't the old religion any more. We wanted to exercise and display our power over stone. We made it into reeds and branches. We squirted it up in all these spires and pinnacles. The priest and his altar were just an excuse. Do you think people have ever feared and worshipped in this—this artist's lark—as they did in Stonehenge?"

"I certainly do not remember that I ever worshipped here," she said.

Sir Richmond was in love with his idea. "The spirit of the Gothic cathedrals," he said, "is the spirit of the sky-scrapers. It is architecture in a mood of flaming ambition. The Freemasons on the building could hardly refrain from jeering at the little priest they had left down below there, performing antiquated puerile mysteries at his altar. He was just their excuse for doing it all.''

"Sky-scrapers?" she conceded. "An early display of the sky-scraper spirit. . . . You are doing your best to make me feel thoroughly at home.''

"You are more at home here still than in that new country of ours over the Atlantic. But it seems to me now that I do begin to remember building this cathedral—and all the other cathedrals we built in Europe. . . . It was the fun of building made us do it. . . .''

"H'm," she said. "And my sky-scrapers?"

"Still the fun of building. That is the thing I envy most about America. It's still large enough, mentally and materially, to build all sorts of things. . . . Over here, the sites are frightfully crowded. . . .''

"And what do you think we are building now? And what do you think you are building over here?''

"What are we building now? I believe we have almost grown up. I believe it is time we began to build in earnest. For good. . . .

"But are we building anything at all?''

"A new world.''

"Show it me," she said.

"We're still only at the foundations," said Sir Richmond. "Nothing shows as yet.''

"I wish I could believe they were foundations."

"But can you doubt we are scrapping the old? . . ."

It was too late in the afternoon to go into the cathedral, so they strolled to and fro round and about the west end and along the path under the trees towards the river, exchanging their ideas very frankly and freely about the things that had recently happened to the world and what they thought they ought to be doing in it.

§ 5

After dinner our four tourists sat late and talked in a corner of the smoking-room. The two ladies had vanished hastily at the first dinner gong and reappeared at the second, mysteriously and pleasantly changed from tweedy pedestrians to indoor company. They were quietly but definitely dressed, pretty alterations had happened to their coiffure, a silver band and deep red stones lit the dusk of Miss Grammont's hair and a necklace of the same colourings kept the peace between her jolly sun-burnt cheek and her soft untanned neck. It was evident her recent uniform had included a collar of great severity. Miss Seyffert had revealed a plump forearm and proclaimed it with a clash of bangles. Dr. Martineau thought her evening throat much too confidential.

The conversation drifted from topic to topic.

It had none of the steady continuity of Sir Richmond's duologue with Miss Grammont. Miss Seyffert's methods were too discursive and exclamatory. She broke every thread that appeared. The *Old George* at Salisbury is really old; it shows it, and Miss Seyffert laced the entire evening with her recognition of the fact. "Just look at that old beam!" she would cry suddenly. "To think it was exactly where it is before there was a Cabot in America!"

Miss Grammont let her companion pull the talk about as she chose. After the animation of the afternoon a sort of lazy contentment had taken possession of the younger lady. She sat deep in a basket chair and spoke now and then. Miss Seyffert gave her impressions of France and Italy. She talked of the cabmen of Naples and the beggars of Amalfi.

Apropos of beggars, Miss Grammont from the depths of her chair threw out the statement that Italy was frightfully overpopulated. "In some parts of Italy it is like mites on a cheese. Nobody seems to be living. Everyone is too busy keeping alive."

"Poor old women carrying loads big enough for mules," said Miss Seyffert.

"Little children working like slaves," said Miss Grammont.

"And everybody begging. Even the people at

work by the roadside. Who ought to be getting wages—sufficient. . . ."

"Begging—from foreigners—is just a sport in Italy," said Sir Richmond. "It doesn't imply want. But I agree that a large part of Italy is frightfully overpopulated. The whole world is. Don't you think so, Martineau?"

"Well—yes—for its present social organization."

"For any social organization," said Sir Richmond.

"I've no doubt of it," said Miss Seyffert, and added amazingly: "I'm out for Birth Control all the time."

A brief but active pause ensued. Dr. Martineau in a state of sudden distress attempted to drink out of a cold and empty coffee cup.

"The world swarms with cramped and undeveloped lives," said Sir Richmond. "Which amount to nothing. Which do not even represent happiness. And which help to use up the resources, the fuel and surplus energy of the world."

"I suppose they have a sort of liking for their lives," Miss Grammont reflected.

"Does that matter? They do nothing to carry life on. They are just vain repetitions—imperfect—dreary, blurred repetitions of one common life. All that they feel has been felt, all that they

do has been done better before. Because they are
crowded and hurried and underfed and undeeredu-
cated. And as for liking their lives, they need
never have had the chance.''

"How many people are there in the world?"
she asked abruptly.

"I don't know. Twelve hundred, fifteen hundred millions perhaps.''

"And in *your* world?"

"I'd have two hundred and fifty millions, let
us say. At most. It would be quite enough for
this little planet, for a time, at any rate. Don't
you think so, doctor?"

"I don't *know*," said Dr. Martineau. "Oddly
enough, I have never thought about that question
before. At least, not from this angle.''

"But could you pick out two hundred and
fifty million aristocrats?'' began Miss Grammont.
"My native instinctive democracy——"

"Need not be outraged,'' said Sir Richmond.
"Any two hundred and fifty million would do,
They'd be able to develop fully, all of them. As
things are, only a minority can do that. The rest
never get a chance.''

"That's what *I* always say,'' said Miss
Seyffert.

"A New Age,'' said Dr. Martineau; "a New
World. We may be coming to such a stage, when
population, as much as fuel, will be under a world
control. If one thing, why not the other? I admit

that the movement of thought is away from haphazard towards control——"

"I'm for control all the time," Miss Seyffert injected, following up her previous success.

"I admit," the doctor began his broken sentence again with marked patience, "that the movement of thought is away from haphazard towards control—in things generally. But is the movement of events?"

"The eternal problem of man," said Sir Richmond. "Can our wills prevail?"

There came a little pause.

Miss Grammont smiled an enquiry at Miss Seyffert. "If *you* are," said Belinda.

"I wish I could imagine your world," said Miss Grammont, rising, "of two hundred and fifty millions of fully developed human beings with room to live and breathe in and no need for wars. Will they live in palaces? Will they all be healthy? . . . Machines will wait on them. No! I can't imagine it. Perhaps I shall dream of it. My dreaming self may be cleverer."

She held out her hand to Sir Richmond. Just for a moment they stood hand in hand, appreciatively. . . .

"Well!" said Dr. Martineau, as the door closed behind the two Americans, "This is a curious—encounter."

"That young woman has brains," said Sir Richmond, standing before the fireplace.

There was no doubt whatever which young woman he meant. But Dr. Martineau grunted.

"I don't like the American type," the doctor pronounced judicially.

"I do," Sir Richmond countered.

The doctor thought for a moment or so. "You are committed to the project of visiting Avebury?" he said.

"They ought to see Avebury," said Sir Richmond.

"H'm," said the doctor, ostentatiously amused by his thoughts and staring at the fire. "Birth Control! I *never* did."

Sir Richmond smiled down on the top of the doctor's head and said nothing.

"I think," said the doctor and paused. . . . "I shall leave this Avebury expedition to you."

"We can be back in the early afternoon," said Sir Richmond. "To give them a chance of seeing the cathedral. The chapter house here is not one to miss. . . ."

"And then I suppose we shall go on?"

"As you please," said Sir Richmond insincerely.

"I must confess that four people make the car at any rate seem tremendously overpopulated. And to tell the truth, I do not find this encounter so amusing as you seem to do. . . . I shall not be sorry when we have waved good-bye to those young ladies, and resume our interrupted conversation."

Sir Richmond considered something mulish in the doctor's averted face.

"I find Miss Grammont an extremely interesting—and stimulating human being."

"Evidently."

The doctor sighed, stood up and found himself delivering one of the sentences he had engendered during his solitary meditations in his room before dinner. He surprised himself by the plainness of his speech. "Let me be frank," he said, regarding Sir Richmond squarely. "Considering the general situation of things and your position, I do not care very greatly for the part of an accessory to what may easily develop, as you know very well, into a very serious—flirtation. An absurd, mischievous, irrelevant flirtation. You may not like the word. You may pretend it is a conversation, an ordinary intellectual conversation. That is not the word. Simply that is not the word. You people eye one another. . . . Flirtation. I give the affair its proper name. That is all. Merely that. When I think—— But we will not discuss it now. . . . Good night. . . . Forgive me if I put before you, rather bluntly, my particular point of view."

Sir Richmond found himself alone. With his eyebrows raised.

§ 6

After twenty-four eventful hours our two students of human motives found themselves together again by the fireplace in the *Old George* smoking-room. They had resumed their overnight conversation, in a state of considerable tension.

"If you find the accommodation of the car insufficient," said Sir Richmond in a tone of extreme reasonableness, "and I admit it is, we can easily hire a larger car in a place like this."

"I would not care if you hired an omnibus," said Dr. Martineau. "I am not coming on if these young women are."

"But if you consider it scandalous—and really, Martineau, really! as one man to another, it does seem to me to be a bit pernickety of you, a broad and original thinker as you are——"

"Thought is one matter. Rash, inconsiderate action quite another. And above all, if I spend another day in or near the company of Miss Belinda Seyffert I shall—I shall be extremely rude to her."

"But," said Sir Richmond and bit his lower lip and considered.

"We might drop Belinda," he suggested—turning to his friend and speaking in low, confidential tones. "She is quite a manageable person. Quite. She could—for example—be left behind with the luggage and sent on by train. I do not know if you realize how the land lies in that quarter. It needs only a word to Miss Grammont.''

There was no immediate reply. For a moment he had a wild hope that his companion would agree, and then he perceived that the doctor's silence meant only the preparation of an ultimatum.

''I object to Miss Grammont and—that side of the thing, more than I do to Miss Seyffert.''

Sir Richmond said nothing.

''It may help you to see this affair from a slightly different angle if I tell you that twice today Miss Seyffert has asked me if you were a married man.''

''And of course you told her I was.''

''On the second occasion.''

Sir Richmond smiled again.

''Frankly,'' said the doctor, ''this adventure is altogether uncongenial to me. It is the sort of thing that has never happened in my life. This highway coupling——''

''Don't you think,'' said Sir Richmond, ''that you are attaching rather too much—what shall I say—romantic?—flirtatious?—meaning to this affair? I don't mind that after my rather lavish confessions you should consider me a rather over-sexed person, but isn't your attitude rather unfair,—unjust, indeed, and almost insulting, to this

Miss Grammont? After all, she's a young lady of very good social position indeed. She doesn't strike you—does she?—as an undignified or helpless human being. Her manners suggest a person of considerable self-control. And knowing less of me than you do, she probably regards me as almost as safe as—a maiden aunt say. I'm twice her age. We are a party of four. There are conventions, there are considerations. . . . Aren't you really, my dear Martineau, overdoing all this side of this very pleasant little enlargement of our interests."

"*Am* I?" said Dr. Martineau and brought a scrutinizing eye to bear on Sir Richmond's face.

"I want to go on talking to Miss Grammont for a day or so," Sir Richmond admitted.

"Then I shall prefer to leave your party."

There were some moments of silence.

"I am really very sorry to find myself in this dilemma," said Sir Richmond with a note of genuine regret in his voice.

"It is not a dilemma," said Dr. Martineau, with a corresponding loss of asperity. "I grant you we discover we differ—upon a question of taste and convenience. But before I suggested this trip, I had intended to spend a little time with my old friend Sir Kenelm Latter at Bournemouth. Nothing simpler than to go to him now. . . ."

"I shall be sorry all the same."

"I could have wished," said the doctor, "that these ladies had happened a little later. . . ."

The matter was settled. Nothing more of a practical nature remained to be said. But neither gentleman wished to break off with a harsh and bare decision.

"When the New Age is here," said Sir Richmond, "then, surely, a friendship between a man and a woman will not be subjected to the—the inconveniences your present code would set about it? They would travel about together as they chose?"

"The fundamental principle of the new age," said the doctor, "will be *Honi soit qui mal y pense*. In these matters. With perhaps *Fay ce que vouldras* as its next injunction. So long as other lives are not affected. In matters of personal behaviour the world will probably be much more free and individuals much more open in their conscience and honour than they have ever been before. In matters of property, economics and public conduct it will probably be just the reverse. Then, there will be much more collective control and much more insistence, legal insistence, upon individual responsibility. But we are not living in a new age yet; we are living in the patched-up ruins of a very old one. And you— if you will forgive me—are living in the patched-up remains of a life that had already had its complications. This young lady, whose charm and cleverness I admit, behaves as if the new age were already here. Well, that may be a very dangerous mistake both for her and for you. . . . This affair, if it goes on for a few days more, may involve very serious consequences indeed, with which I, for one, do not wish to be involved.''

Sir Richmond, upon the hearthrug, had a curious feeling that he was back in the head master's study at Caxton.

Dr. Martineau went on with a lucidity that Sir Richmond found rather trying, to give his impression of Miss Grammont and her position in life.

''She is,'' he said, ''manifestly a very expensively educated girl. And in many ways—interesting. I have been watching her. I have not been favoured with very much of her attention, but that fact has enabled me to see her in profile. Miss Seyffert is a fairly crude mixture of frankness, insincerity and self-explanatory egotism, and I have been able to disregard a considerable amount of the conversation she has addressed to me. Now I guess this Miss Grammont has had no mother since she was quite little.''

''Your guesses, doctor, are apt to be pretty good,'' said Sir Richmond.

''You know that?''

''She has told me as much.''

''H'm. Well—— She impressed me as having the air of a girl who has had to solve many problems for which the normal mother provides ready-made solutions. That is how I inferred that there was no mother. I don't think there has been any stepmother, either friendly or hostile? There hasn't been. I thought not. She has had various governesses and companions, ladies of birth and education, engaged to look after her and she has done exactly what she liked with them. Her manner with Miss Seyffert, an excellent manner for Miss Seyffert, by the bye, isn't the sort of manner anyone acquires in a day. Or for one person only. She is a very sure and commanding young woman.''

Sir Richmond nodded.

''I suppose her father adores and neglects her, and whenever she has wanted a companion or governess butchered, the thing has been done. . . . These business Americans, I am told, neglect their womenkind, give them money and power, let them loose on the world. . . . It is a sort of moral laziness masquerading as affection. . . . Still I suppose custom and tradition kept this girl in her place and she was petted, honoured, amused, talked about but not in a harmful way, and rather bored right up to the time when America came into the war. Theoretically she had a tremendously good time.''

''I think this must be near the truth of her biography,'' said Sir Richmond.

''I suppose she has lovers.''

''You don't mean——?''

"No, I don't. Though that is a matter that ought to have no special interest for you. I mean that she was surrounded by a retinue of men who wanted to marry her or who behaved as though they wanted to marry her or who made her happiness and her gratifications and her condescensions seem a matter of very great importance to them. She had the flattery of an extremely uncritical and unexacting admiration. That is the sort of thing that gratifies a silly woman extremely. Miss Grammont is not silly and all this homage and facile approval probably bored her more than she realized. To anyone too intelligent to be steadily excited by buying things and wearing things and dancing and playing games and going to places of entertainment, and being given flowers, sweets, jewellery, pet animals, and books bound in a special sort of leather, the prospect of being a rich man's only daughter until such time as it becomes advisable to change into a rich man's wealthy wife, is probably not nearly so amusing as envious people might suppose. I take it Miss Grammont had got all she could out of that sort of thing some time before the war, and that she had already read and thought rather more than most young women in her position. Before she was twenty I guess she was already looking for something more interesting in the way of men than a rich admirer with an automobile full of presents. Those who seek find."

"What do you think she found?"

"What would a rich girl find out there in America? I don't know. I haven't the material to guess with. In London a girl might find a considerable variety of active, interesting men, rising politicians, university men of distinction, artists and writers even, men of science, men—there are still such men—active in the creative work of the empire.

"In America I suppose there is at least an equal variety, made up of rather different types. She would find that life was worth while to such people in a way that made the ordinary entertainments and amusements of her life a monstrous silly waste of time. With the facility of her sex she would pick up from one of them the idea that made life worth while for him. I am inclined to think there was someone in her case who did seem to promise a sort of life that was worth while. And that somehow the war came to alter the look of that promise."

"How?"

"I don't know. Perhaps I am only romancing. But for this young woman I am convinced this expedition to Europe has meant—experience, harsh educational experience and very profound mental disturbance. There have been love experiences; experiences that were something more than the treats and attentions and proposals that made up her life when she was sheltered over there.

And something more than that. What it is I don't know. The war has turned an ugly face to her. She has seen death and suffering and ruin. Perhaps she has seen people she knew killed. Perhaps the man has been killed. Or she has met with cowardice or cruelty or treachery where she didn't expect it. She has been shocked out of the first confidence of youth. She has ceased to take the world for granted. . . . It hasn't broken her but it has matured her. . . . That I think is why history has become real to her. Which so attracts you in her. History, for her, has ceased to be a fabric of picturesque incidents; it is the study of a tragic struggle that still goes on. She sees history as you see it and I see it. She is a very grown-up young woman. . . ."

"It's just that," said Sir Richmond. "It's just that. If you see as much in Miss Grammont as all that, why don't you want to come on with us? You see the interest of her."

"I see a lot more than that. You don't know what an advantage it is to be as I am, rather cold and unresponsive to women and unattractive and negligible—negligible, that is the exact word—to them. *You* can't look at a woman for five minutes without losing sight of her in a mist of imaginative excitement. Because she looks back at you. I have the privilege of the negligible—which is a cool head. Miss Grammont has a startled and matured mind, an original mind. Yes. And there is something more to be said. Her intelligence is better than her character.''

''I don't quite see what you are driving at.''

''The intelligence of all intelligent women is better than their characters. Goodness in a woman, as we understand it, seems to imply necessarily a certain imaginative fixity. Miss Grammont has an impulsive and adventurous character. And as I have been saying she was a spoilt child, with no discipline. . . . You also are a person of high intelligence and defective controls. She is very much at loose ends. You—on account of the illness of that rather forgotten lady, Miss Martin Leeds——''

''Aren't you rather abusing the secrets of the confessional?''

''This *is* the confessional. It closes to-morrow morning but it is the confessional still. Look at the thing frankly. You, I say, are also at loose ends. Can you deny it? My dear sir, don't we both know that ever since we left London you have been ready to fall in love with any pretty thing in petticoats that seemed to promise you three ha'porth of kindness. A lost dog looking for a master! You're a stray man looking for a mistress. Miss Grammont being a woman is a little more selective than that. But if she's at a loose end as I suppose, she isn't protected by the sense of having made her selection. And she has no preconceptions of what she wants. You are a very

interesting man in many ways. You carry marriage and—entanglements lightly. With an air of
being neither married nor entangled. She is quite
prepared to fall in love with you."

"But you don't really think that?" said Sir
Richmond, with an ill-concealed eagerness.

Dr. Martineau rolled his face towards Sir Richmond. "These miracles — grotesquely — happen," he said. "She knows nothing of Martin
Leeds. . . . You must remember that. . . .

"And then," he added, "if she and you fall in
love, as the phrase goes, what is to follow?"

There was a pause.

Sir Richmond looked at his toes for a moment
or so as if he took counsel with them and then
decided to take offence.

"Really!" he said, "this is preposterous. You
talk of falling in love as though it was impossible
for a man and woman to be deeply interested in
each other—without that. And the gulf in our
ages—in our quality! From the Psychologist of
a New Age I find this amazing. Are men and
women to go on for ever—separated by this possibility into two hardly communicating and yet
interpenetrating worlds? Is there never to be
friendship and companionship between men and
women without passion?"

"You ought to know even better than I do that
there is not. For such people as you two anyhow.
And at present the world is not prepared to toler-

ate friendship and companionship *with* that accompaniment. That is the core of this situation."

A pause fell between the two gentlemen. They had smoothed over the extreme harshness of their separation and there was very little more to be said.

"Well," said Sir Richmond in conclusion, "I am very sorry indeed, Martineau, that we have to part like this."

CHAPTER THE SEVENTH

COMPANIONSHIP

§ 1

"Well," said Dr. Martineau, extending his hand to Sir Richmond on the Salisbury station platform, "I leave you to it."

His round face betrayed little or no vestiges of his overnight irritation.

"Ought you to leave me to it?" smiled Sir Richmond.

"I shall be interested to learn what happens."

"But if you won't stay to see!"

"Now sir, please," said the guard respectfully but firmly, and Dr. Martineau got in.

Sir Richmond walked thoughtfully down the platform towards the exit.

"What else could I do?" he asked aloud to nobody in particular.

For a little while he thought confusedly of the collapse of his expedition into the secret places of his own heart with Dr. Martineau, and then his prepossession with Miss Grammont resumed possession of his mind. Dr. Martineau was forgotten.

§ 2

For the better part of forty hours, Sir Richmond had either been talking to Miss Grammont, or carrying on imaginary conversations with her in her absence, or sleeping and dreaming dreams in which she never failed to play a part, even if at times it was an altogether amazing and incongruous part. And as they were both very frank and expressive people, they already knew a very great deal about each other.

For an American Miss Grammont was by no means autobiographical. She gave no sketches of her idiosyncrasies, and she repeated no remembered comments and prophets of her contemporaries about herself. She either concealed or she had lost any great interest in her own personality. But she was interested in and curious about the people she had met in life, and her talk of them reflected a considerable amount of light upon her own upbringing and experiences. And her liking for Sir Richmond was pleasingly manifest. She liked his turn of thought, she watched him with a faint smile on her lips as he spoke, and she spread her opinions before him carefully in that soft voice of hers like a shy child showing its treasures to some suddenly trusted and favoured visitor.

Their ways of thought harmonized. They talked at first chiefly about the history of the world and the extraordinary situation of aimlessness in a phase of ruin to which the Great War had brought all Europe, if not all mankind. The world excited them both in the same way; as a crisis in which they were called upon to do something—they did not yet clearly know what. Into this topic they peered as into some deep pool, side by side, and in it they saw each other reflected.

The visit to Avebury had been a great success. It had been a perfect springtime day, and the little inn had been delighted at the reappearance of Sir Richmond's car so soon after its departure. Its delight was particularly manifest in the cream and salad it produced for lunch. Both Miss Grammont and Miss Seyffert displayed an intelligent interest in their food. After lunch they had all gone out to the stones and the wall. Half a dozen sunburnt children were putting one of the partially overturned megaliths to a happy use by clambering to the top of it and sliding on their little behinds down its smooth and sloping side amidst much mirthful squealing.

Sir Richmond and Miss Grammont had walked round the old circumvallation together, but Belinda Seyffert had strayed away from them, professing an interest in flowers. It was not so much that she felt they had to be left together that made her do this as her own consciousness of being possessed by a devil who interrupted conversations.

When Miss Grammont was keenly interested in a conversation, then Belinda had learnt from experience that it was wiser to go off with her devil out of the range of any temptation to interrupt.

"You really think," said Miss Grammont, "that it would be possible to take this confused old world and reshape it, set it marching towards that new world of yours—of two hundred and fifty million fully developed, beautiful and happy people?"

"Why not? Nobody is doing anything with the world except muddle about. Why not give it a direction?"

"You'd take it in your hands like clay?"

"Obdurate clay with a sort of recalcitrant, unintelligent life of its own."

Her imagination glowed in her eyes and warmed her voice. "I believe what you say is possible. If people dare."

"I am tired of following little.motives that are like flames that go out when you get to them. I am tired of seeing all the world doing the same. I am tired of a world in which there is nothing great but great disasters. Here is something mankind can attempt, that we can attempt."

"And will?"

"I believe that as Mankind grows up this is the business Man has to settle down to and will settle down to."

She considered that.

"I've been getting to believe something like

this. But— . . . it frightens me. I suppose most of us have this same sort of dread of taking too much upon ourselves.''

''So we just live like pigs. Sensible little piggy-wiggys. I've got a Committee full of that sort of thing. We live like little modest pigs. And let the world go hang. And pride ourselves upon our freedom from the sin of presumption.''

''Not quite that!''

''Well! How do you put it?''

''We are afraid,'' she said. ''It's too vast. We want bright little lives of our own.''

''Exactly—sensible little piggy-wiggys.''

''We have a right to life—and happiness.''

''First,'' said Sir Richmond, ''as much right as a pig has to food. But whether we get life and happiness or fail to get them we human beings who have imaginations want something more nowadays. . . . Of course we want bright lives, of course we want happiness. Just as we want food, just as we want sleep. But when we have eaten, when we have slept, when we have jolly things about us—it is nothing. We have been made an exception of—and got our rations. The big thing confronts us still. It is vast, I agree, but vast as it is it is the thing we have to think about. I do not know why it should be so, but I am compelled by something in my nature to want to serve this idea of a new age for mankind. I want **it as my culminating** want. I want a world in

order, a disciplined mankind going on to greater
things. Don't you?''

"Now you tell me of it," she said with a smile,
"I do."

"But before——?"

"No. You've made it clear. It wasn't clear
before."

"I've been talking of this sort of thing with
my friend Dr. Martineau. And I've been thinking as well as talking. That perhaps is why I'm
so clear and positive."

"I don't complain that you are clear and positive. I've been coming along the same way. . . .
It's refreshing to meet you."

"I found it refreshing to meet Martineau." A
twinge of conscience about Dr. Martineau turned
Sir Richmond into a new channel. "He's a most
interesting man," he said. "Rather shy in some
respects. Devoted to his work. And he's writing
a book which has saturated him in these ideas.
Only two nights ago we stood here and talked
about it. *The Psychology of a New Age.* The
world, he believes, is entering upon a new phase
in its history, the adolescence, so to speak, of mankind. It is an idea that seizes the imagination.
There is a flow of new ideas abroad, he thinks,
widening realizations, unprecedented hopes and
fears. There is a consciousness of new powers and
new responsibilities. We are sharing the adolescence of our race. It is giving history a new and

more intimate meaning for us. It is bringing us into directer relation with public affairs,—making them matter as formerly they didn't seem to matter. That idea of the bright little private life has to go by the board.''

''I suppose it has,'' she said, meditatively, as though she had been thinking over some such question before.

''The private life,'' she said, ''has a way of coming aboard again.''

Her reflections travelled fast and broke out now far ahead of him.

''You have some sort of work cut out for you,'' she said abruptly.

''Yes. Yes, I have.''

''I haven't,'' she said.

''So that I go about,'' she added, ''like someone who is looking for something. I'd like to know— if it's not jabbing too searching a question at you —what you have found.''

Sir Richmond considered. ''Incidentally,'' he smiled, ''I want to get a lasso over the neck of that very forcible and barbaric person, your father. I am doing my best to help lay the foundation of a scientific world control of fuel production and distribution. We have a Fuel Commission in London with rather wide powers of enquiry into the whole world problem of fuel. We shall come out to Washington presently with proposals.''

Miss Grammont surveyed the landscape. "I suppose," she said, "poor father *is* rather like an unbroken mule in business affairs. So many of our big business men in America are. He'll lash out at you."

"I don't mind if only he lashes out openly in the sight of all men."

She considered and turned on Sir Richmond gravely.

"Tell me what you want to do to him. You find out so many things for me that I seem to have been thinking about in a sort of almost invisible half-conscious way. I've been suspecting for a long time that Civilization wasn't much good unless it got people like my father under some sort of control. But controlling father—as distinguished from managing him!" She reviewed some private and amusing memories. "He is a most intractable man."

§ 3

They had gone on to talk of her father and of the types of men who controlled international business. She had had plentiful opportunities for observation in their homes and her own. Gunter Lake, the big banker, she knew particularly well, because, it seemed, she had been engaged or was engaged to marry him. "All these people," she said, "are pushing things about, affecting millions of lives, hurting and disordering hundreds of thousands of people. They don't seem to know what they are doing. They have no plans in particular. . . . And you are getting something going that will be a plan and a direction and a conscience and a control for them? You will find my father extremely difficult, but some of our younger men would love it.

"And," she went on; "there are American women who'd love it too. We're petted. We're kept out of things. We aren't placed. We don't get enough to do. We're spenders and wasters —not always from choice. While these fathers and brothers and husbands of ours play about with the fuel and power and life and hope of the world as though it was a game of poker. With all the empty unspeakable solemnity of the male. And treat us as though we ought to be satisfied if they bring home part of the winnings.

"That can't go on," she said.

Her eyes went back to the long, low, undulating skyline of the downs. She spoke as though she took up the thread of some controversy that had played a large part in her life. "That isn't going on," she said with an effect of conclusive decision.

Sir Richmond recalled that little speech now as he returned from Salisbury station to the *Old George* after his farewell to Martineau. He recalled too the soft firmness of her profile and the delicate line of her lifted chin. He felt that this

time at any rate he was not being deceived by the
outward shows of a charming human being. This
young woman had real firmness of character to
back up her free and independent judgments. He
smiled at the idea of any facile passion in the composition of so sure and gallant a personality.
Martineau was very fine-minded in many respects,
but he was an old maid; and like all old maids he
saw man and woman in every encounter. But passion was a thing men and women fell back upon
when they had nothing else in common. When
they thought in the pleasantest harmony and
every remark seemed to weave a fresh thread
of common interest, then it wasn't so necessary.
It might happen, but it wasn't so necessary. . . .
If it did it would be a secondary thing to companionship. . . . That's what she was,—a companion.

But a very lovely and wonderful companion, the
companion one would not relinquish until the very
last moment one could keep with her.

Her views about America and about her own
place in the world seemed equally fresh and original to Sir Richmond.

"I realize I've got to be a responsible American
citizen," she had said. That didn't mean that
she attached very much importance to her recently acquired vote. She evidently classified
voters into the irresponsible who just had votes
and the responsible who also had a considerable

amount of property as well. She had no illusions about the power of the former class. It didn't exist. They were steered to their decisions by people employed, directed or stimulated by "father" and his friends and associates, the owners of America, the real "responsible citizens." Or they fell a prey to the merely adventurous leading of "revolutionaries." But anyhow they were steered. She herself, it was clear, was bound to become a very responsible citizen indeed. She would some day, she laughed, be "swimming in oil and suchlike property." Her interest in Sir Richmond's schemes for a scientific world management of fuel was therefore, she realized, a very direct one. But it was remarkable to find a young woman seeing it like that.

Father it seemed varied very much in his attitude towards her. He despised and distrusted women generally, and it was evident he had made it quite clear to her how grave an error it was on her part to persist in being a daughter and not a son. At moments it seemed to Sir Richmond that she was disposed to agree with father upon that. When Mr. Grammont's sense of her regrettable femininity was uppermost, then he gave his intelligence chiefly to schemes for tying her up against the machinations of adventurers by means of trustees, partners, lawyers, advisers, agreements and suchlike complications, or for acquiring a workable son by marriage. To this last idea it would seem the importance in her life of the rather heavily named Gunter Lake was to be ascribed. But another mood of the old man's was distrust of anything that could not be spoken of as his "own flesh and blood," and then he would direct his attention to a kind of masculinization of his daughter and to schemes for giving her the completest control of all he had to leave her provided she never married nor fell under masculine sway. "After all," he would reflect as he hesitated over the practicability of his life's ideal, "there was Hetty Green."

This latter idea had reft her suddenly at the age of seventeen from the educational care of an English gentlewoman warranted to fit her for marriage with any prince in Europe, and thrust her for the mornings and a moiety of the afternoons of the better part of a year, after a swift but competent training, into a shirt waist and an office down town. She had been entrusted at first to a harvester concern independent of Mr. Grammont, because he feared his own people wouldn't train her hard. She had worked for ordinary wages and ordinary hours, and at the end of the day, she mentioned casually, a large automobile with two menservants and a trustworthy secretary used to pick her out from the torrent of undistinguished workers that poured out of the Synoptical Building. This masculinization idea had also sent her on a commission of enquiry into

Mexico. There apparently she had really done responsible work.

But upon the question of labour Mr. Grammont was fierce, even for an American business man, and one night at a dinner party he discovered his daughter displaying what he considered an improper familiarity with socialist ideas. This had produced a violent revulsion towards the purdah system and the idea of a matrimonial alliance with Gunter Lake. Gunter Lake, Sir Richmond gathered, wasn't half a bad fellow. Generally it would seem Miss Grammont liked him, and she had a way of speaking about him that suggested that in some way Mr. Lake had been rather hardly used and had acquired merit by his behaviour under bad treatment. There was some story, however, connected with her war services in Europe upon which Miss Grammont was evidently indisposed to dwell. About that story Sir Richmond was left at the end of his Avebury day and after his last talk with Dr. Martineau, still quite vaguely guessing.

So much fact about Miss Grammont as we have given had floated up in fragments and pieced itself together in Sir Richmond's mind in the course of a day and a half. The fragments came up as allusions or by way of illustration. The sustaining topic was this New Age Sir Richmond foreshadowed, this world under scientific control, the Utopia of fully developed people fully developing

the resources of the earth. For a number of trivial reasons Sir Richmond found himself ascribing
the project of this New Age almost wholly to Dr.
Martineau, and presenting it as a much completer
scheme than he was justified in doing. It was true
that Dr. Martineau had not said many of the
things Sir Richmond ascribed to him, but also it
was true that they had not crystallized out in Sir
Richmond's mind before his talks with Dr. Martineau. The idea of a New Age necessarily carries
with it the idea of fresh rules of conduct and of
different relationships between human beings.
And it throws those who talk about it into the
companionship of a common enterprise. To-morrow the New Age will be here no doubt, but to-
day it is the hope and adventure of only a few
human beings.

So that it was natural for Miss Grammont.and
Sir Richmond to ask: "What are *we* to do with
such types as father?" and to fall into an idiom
that assumed a joint enterprise. They had
agreed by a tacit consent to a common conception
of the world they desired as a world scientifically
ordered, an immense organization of mature commonsense, healthy and secure, gathering knowledge and power for creative adventures as yet
beyond dreaming. They were prepared to think
of the makers of the Avebury dyke as their yesterday selves, of the stone age savages as a
phase in their late childhood, and of this great

world order Sir Richmond foresaw as a day where
dawn was already at hand. And in such long per-
spectives, the states, governments and institutions of to-day became very temporary-looking
and replaceable structures indeed. Both these
two people found themselves thinking in this fashion with an unwonted courage and freedom because the other one had been disposed to think
in this fashion before. Sir Richmond was still
turning over in his mind the happy mutual release of the imagination this chance companionship had brought about when he found himself
back again at the threshold of the *Old George.*

§ 4

Sir Richmond Hardy was not the only man who
was thinking intently about Miss Grammont at
that particular moment. Two gentlemen were
coming towards her across the Atlantic whose
minds, it chanced, were very busily occupied by
her affairs. One of these was her father, who was
lying in his brass bed in his commodious cabin on
the *Hollandia,* regretting his diminishing ability
to sleep in the early morning now, even when he
was in the strong and soothing air of mid-Atlantic,
and thinking of V.V. because she had a way of
coming into his mind when it was undefended; and
the other was Mr. Gunter Lake on the *Megantic,*
one day out from Sandy Hook, who found himself

equally sleepless and preoccupied. And although Mr. Lake was a man of vast activities and complicated engagements he was coming now to Europe for the express purpose of seeing V.V. and having things out with her fully and completely because, in spite of all that had happened, she made such an endless series of delays in coming to America.

Old Grammont as he appeared upon the pillow of his bed by the light of a rose-shaded bedside lamp, was a small-headed, grey-haired gentleman with a wrinkled face and sunken brown eyes. Years of business experience, mitigated only by such exercise as the game of poker affords, had intensified an instinctive inexpressiveness. Under the most solitary circumstances old Grammont was still inexpressive, and the face that stared at the ceiling of his cabin and the problem of his daughter might have been the face of a pickled head in a museum, for any indication it betrayed of the flow of thought within. He lay on his back and his bent knees lifted the bed-clothes into a sharp mountain. He was not even trying to sleep.

Why, he meditated, had V.V. stayed on in Europe so much longer than she need have done? And why had Gunter Lake suddenly got into a state of mind about her? Why didn't the girl confide in her father at least about these things? What was afoot? She had thrown over Lake

once and it seemed she was going to turn him
down again. Well, if she was an ordinary female
person that was a silly sort of thing to do. With
her fortune and his—you could buy the world.
But suppose she was not an ordinary female person. . . . Her mother hadn't been ordinary anyhow, whatever else you called her, and no one
could call Grammont blood an ordinary fluid. . . .
Old Grammont had never had any delusions about
Lake. If Lake's father hadn't been a big man
Lake would never have counted for anything at
all. Suppose she did turn him down. In itself
that wasn't a thing to break her father's heart.

What did matter was not whether she threw
Lake over but what she threw him over for. If
it was because he wasn't man enough, well and
good. But if it was for some other lover, some
good-looking, worthless impostor, some European
title or suchlike folly——!

At the thought of a lover for V.V. a sudden
flood of anger poured across the old man's mind,
behind the still mask of his face. It infuriated
him even to think of V.V., his little V.V., his own
girl, entertaining a lover, being possibly—most
shameful thought—*in love!* Like some ordinary
silly female, sinking to kisses, to the deeds one
could buy and pay for. His V.V.! The idea infuriated and disgusted him. He fought against
it as a possibility. Once some woman in New
York had ventured to hint something to him of

some fellow, some affair with an artist, Caston; she had linked this Caston with V.V.'s red cross nursing in Europe. . . . Old Grammont had made that woman sorry she spoke. Afterwards he had caused enquiries to be made about this Caston, careful enquiries. It seems that he and V.V. had known each other, there had been something —— But nothing that V.V. need be ashamed of. When old Grammont's enquiry man had come back with his report, old Grammont had been very particular about that. At first the fellow had not been very clear, rather muddled indeed as to how things were—no doubt he had wanted to make out there was something just to seem to earn his money. Old Grammont had struck the table sharply and the eyes that looked out of his mask had blazed. "What have you found out against her?" he had asked in a low even voice. "Absolutely nothing, Sir," said the agent, suddenly white to the lips. . . .

Old Grammont stared at his memory of that moment for a while. That affair was all right, quite all right. Of course it was all right. And also, happily, Caston was among the dead. But it was well her broken engagement with Lake had been resumed as though it had never been broken off. If there had been any talk that fact answered it. And now that Lake had served his purpose old Grammont did not care in the least if he was shelved. V.V. could stand alone.

Old Grammont had got a phrase in his mind that looked like dominating the situation. He dreamt of saying to V.V.: "V.V., I'm going to make a man of you—if you're man enough." That was a large proposition; it implied—oh! it implied all sorts of things. It meant that she would care as little for philandering as an able young business man. Perhaps some day, a long time ahead, she might marry. There wasn't much reason for it, but it might be she would not wish to be called a spinster. "Take a husband," thought old Grammont, "when I am gone, as one takes a butler, to make the household complete." In previous meditations on his daughter's outlook old Grammont had found much that was very suggestive in the precedent of Queen Victoria. She had had no husband of the lord and master type, so to speak, but only a Prince Consort, well in hand. Why shouldn't the Grammont heiress dominate her male belonging, if it came to that, in the same fashion? Why shouldn't one tie her up and tie the whole thing up, so far as any male belonging was concerned, leaving V.V. in all other respects free? How could one do it?

The speculative calm of the sunken brown eyes deepened.

His thoughts went back to the white face of the private enquiry agent. "Absolutely nothing, Sir." What had the fellow thought of hinting? Nothing of that kind in V.V.'s composition,—

never fear. Yet it was a curious anomaly that while one had a thousand ways of defending one's daughter and one's property against that daughter's husband, there was no power on earth by which a father could stretch his dead hand between that daughter and the undue influence of a lover. Unless you tied her up for good and all, lover or none. . . .

One was left at the mercy of V.V.'s character. . . .

"I ought to see more of her," he thought. "She gets away from me. Just as her mother did." A man need not suspect his womenkind but he should know what they are doing. It is duty, his protective duty to them. These companions, these Seyffert women and so forth, were all very well in their way; there wasn't much they kept from you if you got them cornered and asked them intently. But a father's eye is better. He must go about with the girl for a time, watch her with other men, give her chances to talk business with him and see if she took them. "V.V., I'm going to make a man of you," the phrase ran through his brain. The deep instinctive jealousy of the primordial father was still strong in old Grammont's blood. It would be pleasant to go about with her on his right hand in Paris, *his* girl, straight and lovely, desirable and unapproachable, —above that sort of nonsense, above all other masculine subjugation.

"V.V., I'm going to make a man of you. . . ."

His mind grew calmer. Whatever she wanted in Paris should be hers. He'd just let her rip. They'd be like sweethearts together, he and his girl.

Old Grammont dozed off into dreamland.

§ 5

The imaginations of Mr. Gunter Lake, two days behind Mr. Grammont upon the Atlantic, were of a gentler, more romantic character. In them V.V. was no longer a daughter in the fierce focus of a father's jealousy, but the goddess enshrined in a good man's heart. Indeed the figure that the limelight of the reverie fell upon was not V.V. at all but Mr. Gunter Lake himself, in his favourite rôle of the perfect lover.

An interminable speech unfolded itself. "I ask for nothing in return. I've never worried you about that Caston business and I never will. Married to me you shall be as free as if you were unmarried. Don't I know, my dear girl, that you don't love me yet. Let that be as you wish. I want nothing you are not willing to give me, nothing at all. All I ask is the privilege of making life happy—and it shall be happy—for you. . . . All I ask. . . . All I ask. . . . Protect, guard, cherish. . . ."

For to Mr. Gunter Lake it seemed there could be no lovelier thing in life than a wife "in name only" slowly warmed into a glow of passion by the steadfast devotion and the strength and wisdom of a mate at first despised. Until at last a day would come. . . .

"My darling!" Mr. Gunter Lake whispered to the darkness. "My little guurl. *It has been worth the waiting. . . .*"

§ 6

Miss Grammont met Sir Richmond in the bureau of the *Old George* with a telegram in her hand. "My father reported his latitude and longitude by wireless last night. The London people think he will be off Falmouth in four days' time. He wants me to join his liner there and go on to Cherbourg and Paris. He's arranged that. He's the sort of man who can arrange things like that. There'll be someone at Falmouth to look after us and put us aboard the liner. I must wire them where I can pick up a telegram to-morrow."

"Wells in Somerset," said Sir Richmond.

His plans were already quite clear. He explained that he wanted her first to see Shaftesbury, a little old Wessex town that was three or four hundred years older than Salisbury, perched on a hill, a Saxon town, where Alfred had gathered his forces against the Danes and where Canute,

who had ruled over all Scandinavia and Iceland
and Greenland, and had come near ruling a patch
of America, had died. It was a little sleepy place
now, looking out dreamily over beautiful views.
They would lunch in Shaftesbury and walk round
it. Then they would go in the afternoon through
the pleasant west country where the Celts had pre-
vailed against the old folk of the Stonehenge tem-
ple and the Romans against the Celts and the
Saxons against the Romanized Britons and the
Danes against the Saxons, a war-scarred landscape, abounding in dykes and entrenchments and
castles, sunken now into the deepest peace, to
Glastonbury to see what there was to see of a
marsh village the Celts had made for themselves
three or four hundred years before the Romans
came. And at Glastonbury also there were the
ruins of a great Benedictine church and abbey
that had once rivalled Salisbury. Thence they
would go on to Wells to see yet another great
cathedral and to dine and sleep. Glastonbury
Abbey and Wells Cathedral brought the story of
Europe right up to Reformation times.

"That will be a good day for us," said Sir
Richmond. "It will be like turning over the pages
of the history of our family, to and fro. There
will be nothing nearly so old as Avebury in it,
but there will be something from almost every
chapter that comes after Stonehenge. Rome will
be poorly represented, but that may come the day

after at Bath. And the next day too I want to show you something of our old River Severn. We will come right up to the present if we go through Bristol. There we shall have a whiff of America, our new find, from which the tobacco comes, and we shall be reminded of how we set sail thither—was it yesterday or the day before? You will understand at Bristol how it is that the energy has gone out of this dreaming land—to Africa and America and the whole wide world. It was the good men of Bristol, by the bye, with their trade from Africa to America, who gave you your colour problem. Bristol we may go through to-morrow and Gloucester, mother of I don't know how many American Gloucesters. Bath we'll get in somehow. And then as an Anglo-American showman I shall be tempted to run you northward a little way past Tewkesbury, just to go into a church here and there and show you monuments bearing little shields with the stars and stripes upon them, a few stars and a few stripes, the Washington family monuments.''

"It was not only from England that America came,'' said Miss Grammont.

"But England takes an American memory back most easily and most fully—to Avebury and the Baltic Northmen, past the emperors and the Corinthian columns that smothered Latin Europe. . . . For you and me anyhow this is our past, this was our childhood, and this is our land.''

He interrupted laughing as she was about to reply. "Well, anyhow," he said, "it is a beautiful day and a pretty country before us with the ripest history in every grain of its soil. So we'll send a wire to your London people and tell them to send their instructions to Wells."

"I'll tell Belinda," she said, "to be quick with her packing."

§ 7

As Miss Grammont and Sir Richmond Hardy fulfilled the details of his excellent programme and revised their impressions of the past and their ideas about the future in the springtime sunlight of Wiltshire and Somerset, with Miss Seyffert acting the part of an almost ostentatiously discreet chorus, it was inevitable that their conversation should become, by imperceptible gradations, more personal and intimate. They kept up the pose, which was supposed to represent Dr. Martineau's philosophy, of being Man and Woman on their Planet considering its Future, but insensibly they developed the idiosyncrasies of their position. They might profess to be Man and Woman in the most general terms, but the facts that she was the daughter not of Everyman but old Grammont and that Sir Richmond was the angry leader of a minority upon the Fuel Commission became more and more important. "What shall

we do with this planet of ours?'' gave way by
the easiest transitions to "What are you and I
doing and what have we got to do? How do you
feel about it all? What do you desire and what
do you dare?''

It was natural that Sir Richmond should talk
of his Fuel Commission to a young woman whose
interests in fuel were even greater than his own.
He found that she was very much better read than
he was in the recent literature of socialism, and
that she had what he considered to be a most
unfeminine grasp of economic ideas. He thought
her attitude towards socialism a very sane one
because it was also his own. So far as socialism
involved the idea of a scientific control of natural
resources as a common property administered in
the common interest, she and he were very greatly
attracted by it; but so far as it served as a form
of expression for the merely insubordinate discontent of the many with the few, under any conditions, so long as it was a formula for class jealousy and warfare, they were both repelled by it.
If she had had any illusions about the working
class possessing as a class any profounder political wisdom or more generous public impulses
than any other class, those illusions had long since
departed. People were much the same, she
thought, in every class; there was no stratification
of either rightness or righteousness.

He found he could talk to her of his work and

aims upon the Fuel Commission and of the conflict and failure of motives he found in himself, as freely as he had done to Dr. Martineau and with a surer confidence of understanding. Perhaps his talks with the doctor had got his ideas into order and made them more readily expressible than they would have been otherwise. He argued against the belief that any class could be good as a class or bad as a class, and he instanced the conflict of motives he found in all the members of his Committee and most so in himself. He repeated the persuasion he had already confessed to Dr. Martineau that there was not a single member of the Fuel Commission but had a considerable drive towards doing the right thing about fuel, and not one who had a single-minded, unencumbered drive towards the right thing. "That," said Sir Richmond, "is what makes life so interesting and, in spite of a thousand tragic disappointments, so hopeful. Every man is a bad man, every man is a feeble man and every man is a good man. My motives come and go. Yours do the same. We vary in response to the circumstances about us. Given a proper atmosphere, most men will be public-spirited, right-living, generous. Given perplexities and darkness, most of us can be cowardly and vile. People say you cannot change human nature and perhaps that is true, but you can change its responses endlessly. The other day I was in Bohemia, discussing Silesian

coal with Benes, and I went to see the Festival of
the Bohemian Sokols. Opposite to where I sat,
far away across the arena, was a great bank of
men of the Sokol organizations, an unbroken
brown mass wrapped in their brown uniform
cloaks. Suddenly the sun came out and at a
word the whole body flung back their cloaks,
showed their Garibaldi shirts and became one
solid blaze of red. It was an amazing transforma-
tion until one understood what had happened.
Yet nothing material had changed—but the sunshine. And given a change in laws and prevailing
ideas, and the very same people who are greedy
traders, grasping owners and revolting workers
to-day will all throw their cloaks aside and you
will find them working together cheerfully, even
generously, for a common end. They aren't traders and owners and workers and so forth by any
inner necessity. Those are just the ugly parts
they play in the present drama. Which is nearly
at the end of its run."

"That's a hopeful view," said Miss Grammont.
"I don't see the flaw in it—if there is a flaw."

"There isn't one," said Sir Richmond. "It is
my chief discovery about life. I began with the
question of fuel and the energy it affords mankind, and I have found that my generalization applies to all human affairs. Human beings are
fools, weaklings, cowards, passionate idiots,—I
grant you. That is the brown cloak side of them,

so to speak. But they are not such fools and so forth that they can't do pretty well materially if once we hammer out a sane collective method of getting and using fuel. Which people generally will understand—in the place of our present methods of snatch and wrangle. Of that I am absolutely convinced. Some work, some help, some willingness you can get out of everybody. That's the red. And the same principle applies to most labour and property problems, to health, to education, to population, social relationships and war and peace. We haven't got the right system, we have inefficient half-baked systems, or no system at all, and a wild confusion and war of ideas in all these respects. But there is a right system possible none the less. Let us only hammer our way through to the sane and reasonable organization in this and that and the other human affairs, and once we have got it, we shall have got it for good. We may not live to see even the beginnings of success, but the spirit of order, the spirit that has already produced organized science, if only there are a few faithful, persistent people to stick to the job, will in the long run certainly save mankind and make human life— clean and splendid, happy work in a clear mind. If I could live to see it!''

"And as for us—in our time?"

"Measured by the end we serve, we don't matter. You know we don't matter."

"We have to find our fun in the building and in our confidence that we do really build."

"So long as our confidence lasts there is no great hardship," said Sir Richmond.

"So long as our confidence lasts," she repeated after him.

"Ah!" cried Sir Richmond. "There it is! So long as our confidence lasts! So long as one keeps one's mind steady. That is what I came away with Dr. Martineau to discuss. I went to him for advice. I haven't known him for more than a month. It's amusing to find myself preaching forth to you. It was just faith I had lost. Suddenly I had lost my power of work. My confidence in the rightness of what I was doing evaporated. My will failed me. I don't know if you will understand what that means. It wasn't that my reason didn't assure me just as certainly as ever that what I was trying to do was the right thing to try to do. But somehow that seemed a cold and personally unimportant proposition. The life had gone out of it. . . ."

He paused as if arrested by a momentary doubt. "I don't know why I tell you these things," he said.

"You tell them me," she said.

"It's a little like a patient in a hydropath retailing his ailments."

"No. No. Go on."

"I began to think now that what took the go

out of me as my work went on was the lack of any real fellowship in what I was doing. It was the pressure of the opposition in the Committee, day after day. It was being up against men who didn't reason against me but who just showed by everything they did that the things I wanted to achieve didn't matter to them one rap. It was going back to a home, lunching in clubs, reading papers, going about a world in which all the organization, all the possibility of the organization I dream of is tacitly denied. I don't know if it seems an extraordinary confession of weakness to you, but that steady refusal of the majority of my Committee to come into co-operation with me has beaten me—or at any rate has come very near to beating me. Most of them you know are such *able* men. You can *feel* their knowledge and commonsense. They, and everybody about me, seemed busy and intent upon more immediate things, that seemed more real to them than this remote, theoretical, *priggish* end I have set for myself. . . ."

He paused.

"Go on," said Miss Grammont. "I think I understand this."

"And yet I know I am right."

"I know you are right. I'm certain. Go on."

"If one of those ten thousand members of the Sokol Society had thrown back his brown cloak and shown red when all the others still kept them-

selves cloaked—if he was a normal sensitive man
—he might have felt something of a fool. He
might have felt premature and presumptuous.
Red he was and the others he knew were red also,
but why show it? That is the peculiar distress of
people like ourselves, who have some sense of
history and some sense of a larger life within us
than our merely personal life. We don't want
to go on with the old story merely. We want to
live somehow in that larger life and to live for
its greater ends and lose something unbearable
of ourselves, and in wanting to do that we are only
wanting to do what nearly everybody perhaps is
ripe to do and will presently want to do. When
the New Age Martineau talks about begins to
come it may come very quickly—as the red came
at Prague. But for the present everyone hesi-
tates about throwing back the cloak.''

''Until the cloak becomes unbearable,'' she said,
repeating his word.

''I came upon this holiday in the queerest
state. I thought I was ill. I thought I was overworked. But the real trouble was a loneliness that
robbed me of all driving force. Nobody seemed
thinking and feeling with me. . . . I have never
realized until now what a gregarious beast man
is. It needed only a day or so with Martineau,
in the atmosphere of ideas and beliefs like my
own, to begin my restoration. Now as I talk to
you—— That is why I have clutched at your

company. Because here you are, coming from thousands of miles away, and you talk my ideas, you fall into my ways of thought as though we had gone to the same school."

"Perhaps we *have* gone to the same school," she said.

"You mean?"

"Disappointment. Disillusionment. Having to find something better in life than the first things it promised us."

"But you——? Disappointed? I thought that in America people might be educating already on different lines——"

"Even in America," Miss Grammont said, "crops only grow on the ploughed land."

§ 8

Glastonbury in the afternoon was wonderful; they talked of Avalon and of that vanished legendary world of King Arthur and his knights, and in the early evening they came to Wells and a pleasant inn, with a quaint little garden before its front door that gave directly upon the cathedral. The three tourists devoted a golden half hour before dinner to the sculptures on the western face. The great screen of wrought stone rose up warmly, grey and clear and distinct against a clear blue sky in which the moon hung, round and

mendously excited. . . . And at the same time I dreaded the enormous interference. . . .

"I wasn't temperamentally a cold girl. Men interested and excited me, but there were a lot of men about and they clashed with each other. Perhaps way down in some out of the way place I should have fallen in love quite easily with the one man who came along. But no man fixed his image. After a year or so I think I began to lose the power which is natural to a young girl of falling very easily into love. I became critical of the youths and men who were attracted to me and I became analytical about myself. . . .

"I suppose it is because you and I are going to part so soon that I can speak so freely to you. . . . But there are things about myself that I have never had out even with myself. I can talk to myself in you——"

She paused baffled. "I know exactly," said Sir Richmond.

"In my composition I perceive there have always been two ruling strains. I was a spoilt child at home, a rather reserved girl at school, keen on my dignity. I liked respect. I didn't give myself away. I suppose one would call that personal pride. Anyhow it was that streak made me value the position of being a rich married woman in New York. That was why I became engaged to Lake. He seemed to be as good a man as there was about. He said he adored me and

wanted me to crown his life. He wasn't ill-look-
ing or ill-mannered. The second main streak in
my nature wouldn't however fit in with that."

She stopped short.

"The second streak," said Sir Richmond.

"Oh!—— Love of beauty, love of romance. I
want to give things their proper names; I don't
want to pretend to you. . . . It was more or less
than that. . . . It was—imaginative sensuous-
ness. Why should I pretend it wasn't in me? I
believe that streak is in all women."

"I believe so too. In all properly constituted
women."

"I tried to devote that streak to Lake," she
said. "I did my best for him. But Lake was
much too much of a gentleman or an idealist.about
women, or what you will, to know his business as
a lover. And that side of me fell in love, the
rest of me protesting, with a man named Caston.
It was a notorious affair. Everybody in New
York couples my name with Caston. Except when
my father is about. His jealousy has blasted a
area of silence—in that matter—all round him.
He will not know of that story. And they dare
not tell him. I should pity anyone who tried to
tell it him."

"What sort of man was this Caston?"

Miss Grammont seemed to consider. She did
not look at Sir Richmond; she kept her profile to
him.

"He was," she said deliberately, "a very rotten sort of man."

She spoke like one resolved to be exact and judicial. "I believe I always knew he wasn't right. But he was very handsome. And ten years younger than Lake. And nobody else seemed to be all right, so I swallowed that. He was an artist, a painter. Perhaps you know his work." Sir Richmond shook his head. "He could make American business men look like characters out of the Three Musketeers, they said, and he was beginning to be popular. He made love to me. In exactly the way Lake didn't. If I shut my eyes to one or two things, it was delightful. I liked it. But my father would have stood a painter as my husband almost as cheerfully as he would a man of colour. I made a fool of myself, as people say, about Caston. Well—— When the war came, he talked in a way that irritated me. He talked like an East Side Annunzio, about art and war. It made me furious to know it was all talk and that he didn't mean business. . . . I made him go."

She paused for a moment. "He hated to go.

"Then I relented. Or I missed him and I wanted to be made love to. Or I really wanted to go on my own account. I forget. I forget my motives altogether now. That early war time was a queer time for everyone. A kind of wildness got into the blood. . . . I threw over Lake. All

the time things had been going on in New York—
I had still been engaged to Lake. I went to
France. I did good work. I did do good work.
And also things were possible that would have
seemed fantastic in America. You know something of the war-time atmosphere. There was
death everywhere and people snatched at gratifications. Caston made 'To-morrow we die' his text.
We contrived three days in Paris together—not
very cleverly. All sorts of people know about it.
. . . We went very far."

She stopped short.

"Well?" said Sir Richmond.

"He did die. . . ."

Another long pause. "They told me Caston
had been killed. But someone hinted—or I
guessed—that there was more in it than an ordinary casualty.

"Nobody, I think, realizes that I know. This
is the first time I have ever confessed that I
do know. He was shot. He was shot for
cowardice."

"That might happen to any man," said Sir
Richmond presently. "No man is a hero all
round the twenty-four hours. Perhaps he was
caught by circumstances, unprepared. He may
have been taken by surprise."

"It was the most calculated, cold-blooded cowardice imaginable. He let three other men go on
and get killed. . . .

"No. It is no good your inventing excuses for a man you know nothing about. It was vile, contemptible cowardice—and meanness. It fitted in with a score of ugly little things I remembered. It explained them all. I know the evidence and the judgment against him were strictly just and true, because they were exactly in character. . . . And that, you see, was my man. That was the lover I had chosen. That was the man to whom I had given myself with both hands."

Her soft unhurrying voice halted for a time, and then resumed in the same even tones of careful statement. "I wasn't disgusted, not even with myself. About him I was chiefly sorry, intensely sorry, because I had made him come out of a life that suited and protected him, to the war. About myself, I was stunned and perplexed. I had the clearest realization that what you and I have been calling the bright little personal life had broken off short and was spoilt and over and done with. I felt as though it was my body they had shot. And there I was, with fifty years of life left in me and nothing particular to do with them."

"That was just the prelude to life," said Sir Richmond.

"It didn't seem so at the time. I felt I had to get hold of something or go to pieces. I couldn't turn to religion. I had no religion. And Duty? What is Duty? I set myself to that. I had a kind

of revelation one night. 'Either I find out what
all this world is about,' I said, 'or I perish.' I
have lost myself and I must forget myself—by
getting hold of something bigger than myself.
And becoming that. That's why I have been making a sort of historical pilgrimage. . . . That's
my story, Sir Richmond. That's my education.
. . . Somehow though your troubles are different,
it seems to me that my little muddle makes me understand how it is with you. What you've got,
this idea of a scientific ordering of the world, is
what I, in my younger, less experienced way, have
been feeling my way towards. I want to join on.
I want to get hold of this idea of a great fuel control in the world and of a still greater economic
and educational control of which it is a part. I
want to make that idea a part of myself. Rather I
want to make myself a part of it. When you talk
of it I believe in it altogether."

"And I believe in it, when I talk of it to you."

§ 9

Sir Richmond was stirred very deeply by Miss
Grammont's confidences. His dispute with Dr.
Martineau was present in his mind, so that he
did not want to make love to her. But he was extremely anxious to express his vivid sense of the
value of her friendship. And while he hesitated
over this difficult and unfamiliar task she began

to talk again of herself, and in such a way as to
give a new turn to Sir Richmond's thoughts.

"Perhaps I ought to tell you a little more about
myself," she said; "now that I have told you so
much. I did a thing that still puzzles me. I was
filled with a sense of hopeless disaster in France
and I suppose I had some sort of desperate idea
of saving something out of the situation. . . . I
renewed my correspondence with Gunter Lake.
He made the suggestion I knew he would make,
and I renewed our engagement."

"To go back to wealth and dignity in New
York?"

"Yes."

"But you don't love him?"

"That's always been plain to me. But what I
didn't realize, until I had given my promise over
again, was that I dislike him—acutely."

"You hadn't realized that before?"

"I hadn't thought about him sufficiently. But
now I had to think about him a lot. The other
affair had given me an idea perhaps of what it
means to be married to a man. And here I am
drifting back to him. The horrible thing about
him is the steady—*enveloping* way in which he
has always come at me. Without fellowship.
Without any community of ideas. Ready to make
the most extraordinary bargains. So long as he
can in any way fix me and get me. What does it
mean? What is there behind those watching,

soliciting eyes of his? I don't in the least love him, and this desire and service and all the rest of it he offers me—it's not love. It's not even such love as Caston gave me. It's a game he plays with his imagination.''

She had released a flood of new ideas in Sir Richmond's mind. ''This is—illuminating,'' he said. ''You dislike Lake acutely. You always have disliked him.''

''I suppose I have. But it's only now I admit it to myself.''

''Yes. And—— You might, for example, have married him in New York before the war.''

''It came very near to that.''

''And then probably you wouldn't have discovered you disliked him. You wouldn't have admitted it to yourself.''

''I suppose I shouldn't. I suppose I should have tried to believe I loved him.''

''Women do this sort of thing. Odd! I never realized it before. And there are endless wives suppressing an acute dislike. My wife does. I see now quite clearly that she detests me. Reasonably enough. From her angle I'm entirely detestable. But she won't admit it, won't know of it. She never will. To the end of my life, always, she will keep that detestation unconfessed. She puts a face on the matter. We both do. And this affair of yours. . . . Have you thought how unjust it is to Lake?''

"Not nearly so much as I might have done."

"It is unfair to him. Atrociously unfair. He's not my sort of man, perhaps, but it will hurt him cruelly according to the peculiar laws of his being. He seems to me a crawling sort of lover— with an immense self-conceit at the back of his crawlingness."

"He has," she endorsed.

"He backs himself to crawl—until he crawls triumphantly right over you. . . . I don't like to think of the dream he has. . . . I take it he will lose. Is it fair to go into this game with him?"

"In the interests of Lake," she said, smiling softly at Sir Richmond in the moonlight. "But you are perfectly right."

"And suppose he doesn't lose!"

Sir Richmond found himself uttering sentiments.

"There is only one decent way in which a civilized man and a civilized woman may approach one another. Passionate desire is not enough. What is called love is not enough. Pledges, rational considerations, all these things are worthless. All these things are compatible with hate. The primary essential is friendship, clear understanding, absolute confidence. Then within that condition, in that elect relationship, love is permissible, mating, marriage or no marriage, as you will—all things are permissible. . . ."

Came a long pause between them.

"Dear old cathedral," said Miss Grammont, a little irrelevantly. She had an air of having concluded something that to Sir Richmond seemed scarcely to have begun. She stood looking at the great dark façade edged with moonlight for some moments, and then turned towards the hotel, which showed a pink-lit window.

"I wonder," she said, "if Belinda is still up. And what she will think when I tell her of the final extinction of Mr. Lake. I think she rather looked forward to being the intimate friend, secrets and everything, of Mrs. Gunter Lake."

§ 10

Sir Richmond woke up at dawn and he woke out of an extraordinary dream. He was saying to Miss Grammont: "There is no other marriage than the marriage of true minds. There is no other marriage than the marriage of true minds." He saw her as he had seen her the evening before, light and cool, coming towards him in the moonlight from the hotel. But also in the inconsistent way of dreams he was very close to her kind, faintly smiling face, and his eyes were wet with tears and he was kissing her hand. "My dear wife and mate," he was saying, and suddenly he was kissing her cool lips.

He woke up and stared at his dream, which faded out only very slowly before the fresh sunrise upon the red tiles and tree boughs outside the open window, and before the first stir and clamour of the birds.

He felt like a court in which some overwhelmingly revolutionary piece of evidence had been tendered. All the elaborate defence had broken down at one blow. He sat up on the edge of his bed, facing the new fact.

"This is monstrous and ridiculous," he said, "and Martineau judged me exactly. I am in love with her. . . . I am head over heels in love with her. I have never been so much in love or so truly in love with anyone before."

§ 11

That was the dawn of a long day of tension for Sir Richmond and Miss Grammont. Because each was now vividly aware of being in love with the other and so neither was able to see how things were with the other. They were afraid of each other. A restraint had come upon them both, a restraint that was greatly enhanced by their sense of Belinda, acutely observant, ostentatiously tactful and self-effacing, and prepared at the slightest encouragement to be overwhelmingly romantic and sympathetic. Their talk waned, and was revived to an artificial activity and waned again. The historical interest had evaporated from the west of England and left only an urgent and embarrassing present.

But the loveliness of the weather did not fail, and the whole day was set in Severn landscapes. They first saw the great river like a sea with the Welsh mountains hanging in the sky behind as they came over the Mendip crest above Shipham. They saw it again as they crossed the hill before Clifton Bridge, and so they continued, climbing to hill crests for views at Alveston and near Dursley, and so to Gloucester and the lowest bridge and thence back down stream again through fat meadow lands at first and much apple-blossom and then over gentle hills through wide, pale Newnham and Lidney and Alvington and Woolaston to old Chepstow and its brown castle, always with the widening estuary to the left of them and its foaming shoals and shining sand banks. From Chepstow they turned back north along the steep Wye gorge to Tintern, and there at the snug little Beaufort Arms with its prim lawn and flower garden they ended the day's journey.

Tintern Abbey they thought a poor graceless mass of ruin down beside the river, and it was fenced about jealously and locked up from their invasion. After dinner Sir Richmond and Miss Grammont went for a walk in the mingled twilight and moonlight up the hill towards Chepstow. Both of them were absurdly and nervously pressing to Belinda to come with them, but she was far too

wise to take this sudden desire for her company
seriously. Her dinner shoes, she said, were too
thin. Perhaps she would change and come out a
little later. "Yes, come later," said Miss Grammont and led the way to the door.

They passed through the garden. "I think we
go up the hill?" said Sir Richmond.

"Yes," she agreed, "up the hill."

Followed a silence.

Sir Richmond made an effort, but after some
artificial and disconnected talk about Tintern
Abbey, concerning which she had no history ready,
and then, still lamer, about whether Monmouth-
shire is in England or Wales, silence fell again.
The silence lengthened, assumed a significance, a
dignity that no common words might break.

Then Sir Richmond spoke. "I love you," he
said, "with all my heart."

Her soft voice came back after a stillness. "I
love you," she said, "with all myself."

"I had long ceased to hope," said Sir Richmond,
"that I should ever find a friend . . . a lover
. . . perfect companionship. . . ."

They went on walking side by side, without
touching each other or turning to each other.

"All the things I wanted to think I believe
have come alive in me," she said. . . .

"Cool and sweet," said Sir Richmond. "Such
happiness as I could not have imagined."

The light of a silent bicycle appeared above

them up the hill and swept down upon them, lit their two still faces brightly and passed.

"My dear," she whispered in the darkness between the high hedges.

They stopped short and stood quite still, trembling. He saw her face, dim and tender, looking up to his.

Then he took her in his arms and kissed her lips as he had desired in his dream. . . .

When they returned to the inn Belinda Seyffert offered flat explanations of why she had not followed them, and enlarged upon the moonlight effect of the Abbey ruins from the inn lawn. But the scared congratulations in her eyes betrayed her recognition that momentous things had happened between the two.

CHAPTER THE EIGHTH

Full Moon

§ 1

Sir Richmond had talked in the moonlight and
shadows of having found such happiness as he
could not have imagined. But when he awoke in
the night that happiness had evaporated. He
awoke suddenly out of this love dream that had
lasted now for nearly four days and he awoke in
a mood of astonishment and dismay.

He had thought that when he parted from Dr.
Martineau he had parted also from that process
of self-exploration that they had started together,
but now he awakened to find it established and in
full activity in his mind. Something or someone,
a sort of etherealized Martineau-Hardy, an ab-
stracted intellectual conscience, was demanding
what he thought he was doing with Miss Grammont and whither he thought he was taking her,
how he proposed to reconcile the close relationship
with her that he was now embarked upon with,
in the first place, his work upon and engagements
with the Fuel Commission, and, in the second
place, Martin Leeds. Curiously enough Lady

221

Hardy didn't come into the case at all. He had done his utmost to keep Martin Leeds out of his head throughout the development of this affair. Now in an unruly and determined way that was extremely characteristic of her she seemed resolute to break in.

She appeared as an advocate, without affection for her client but without any hostility, of the claims of Miss Grammont to be let alone. The elaborate pretence that Sir Richmond had maintained to himself that he had not made love to Miss Grammont, that their mutual attraction had been irresistible and had achieved its end in spite of their resolute and complete detachment, collapsed and vanished from his mind. He admitted to himself that driven by a kind of instinctive necessity he had led their conversation step by step to a realization and declaration of love, and that it did not exonerate him in the least that Miss Grammont had been quite ready and willing to help him and meet him half way. She wanted love as a woman does, more than a man does, and he had steadily presented himself as a man free to love, able to love and loving.

"She wanted a man to love, she wanted perfected fellowship, and you have made her that tremendous promise. That was implicit in your embrace. And how can you keep that promise?"

It was as if Martin spoke; it was her voice; it was the very quality of her thought.

"You belong to this work of yours, which must needs be interrupted or abandoned if you take her. Whatever is not mortgaged to your work is mortgaged to me. For the strange thing in all this is that you and I love one another—and have no power to do otherwise. In spite of all this.

"You have nothing to give her but stolen goods," said the shadow of Martin. "You have nothing to give anyone personally any more. . . .

"Think of the love that she desires and think of this love that you can give. . . .

"Is there any new thing in you that you can give her that you haven't given me? You and I know each other very well; perhaps I know *you* too well. Haven't you loved me as much as you can love anyone? Think of all that there has been between us that you are ready now, eager now to set aside and forget as though it had never been. For four days you have kept me out of your mind in order to worship her. Yet you have known I was there—for all you would not know. No one else will ever be so intimate with you as I am. We have quarrelled together, wept together, jested happily and jested bitterly. You have spared me not at all. Pitiless and cruel you have been to me. You have reckoned up all my faults against me as though they were sins. You have treated me at times unlovingly—never was lover treated so un- lovingly as you have sometimes treated me. And yet I have your love—as no other woman can ever have it. Even now when you are wildly in love with this girl's freshness and boldness and cleverness I come into your mind by right and necessity.

"She is different," argued Sir Richmond.

"But you are the same," said the shadow of Martin with Martin's unsparing return. "Your love has never been a steadfast thing. It comes and goes—like the wind. You are an extravagantly imperfect lover. But I have learnt to accept you, as people accept the English weather. . . . Never in all your life have you loved, wholly, fully, steadfastly—as people deserve to be loved; not your mother nor your father, not your wife nor your children, nor me, nor our child, nor any living thing. Pleasant to all of us at times—at times bitterly disappointing. You do not even love this work of yours steadfastly, this work to which you sacrifice us all in turn. You do not love enough. That is why you have these moods and changes, that is why you have these lassitudes. So it is you are made. . . .

"And that is why you must not take this brave young life, so much simpler and braver than your own, and exalt it—as you can do—and then fail it, as you will do. . . ."

Sir Richmond's mind and body lay very still for a time.

"Should I fail her? . . ."

For a time Martin Leeds passed from the foreground of his mind.

He was astonished to think how planless, instinctive and unforeseeing his treatment of Miss Grammont had been. It had been just a blind drive to get hold of her and possess her. . . .

Suddenly his passion for her became active in its defence again.

"But is there such a thing as a perfect love? Is *yours* a perfect love, my dear Martin, with its insatiable jealousy, its ruthless criticism? Has the world ever seen a perfect lover yet? Isn't it our imperfection that brings us together in a common need? Is Miss Grammont, after all, likely to get a more perfect love in all her life than this poor love of mine? And isn't it good for her that she should love?"

"Perfect love cherishes. Perfect love foregoes."

Sir Richmond found his mind wandering far away from the immediate question. "Perfect love," the phrase was his point of departure. Was it true that he could not love passionately and completely? Was that fundamentally what was the matter with him? Was that perhaps what was the matter with the whole world of mankind? It had not yet come to that power of loving which makes action full and simple and direct and unhesitating. Man upon his planet has not grown up to love, is still an eager, egotistical and fluctuating adolescent. He lacks the courage to love and the wisdom to love. Love is here. But it comes and goes, it is mixed with greeds and jealousies and cowardice and cowardly reservations. One hears it only in snatches and single notes. It is like something tuning up before the music begins. . . . The metaphor altogether ran away with Sir Richmond's half dreaming mind. Some day perhaps all life would go to music.

Love was music and power. If he had loved enough he need never have drifted away from his wife. Love would have created love, would have tolerated and taught and inspired. Where there is perfect love there is neither greed nor impatience. He would have done his work calmly. He would have won his way with his Committee instead of fighting and quarrelling with it perpetually. . . .

"Flimsy creatures," he whispered. "Uncertain health. Uncertain strength. A will that comes and goes. Moods of baseness. Moods of utter beastliness. . . . Love like April sunshine. April? . . ."

He dozed and dreamt for a time of spring passing into a high summer sunshine, into a continuing music, of love. He thought of a world like some great playhouse in which players and orchestra and audience all co-operate in a noble production without dissent or conflict. He thought he was the savage of thirty thousand years ago dreaming of the great world that is still perhaps thirty thousand years ahead. His effort to see more of

that coming world than indistinct and cloudy
pinnacles and to hear more than a vague music,
dissolved his dream and left him awake again and
wrestling with the problem of Miss Grammont.

§ 2

The shadow of Martin stood over him, inexor-
able. He had to release Miss Grammont from the
adventure into which he had drawn her. This decision stood out stern and inevitable in his mind
with no conceivable alternative.

As he looked at the task before him he began
to realize its difficulty. He was profoundly in
love with her, he was still only learning how
deeply, and she was not going to play a merely
passive part in this affair. She was perhaps as
deeply in love with him. . . .

He could not bring himself to the idea of confessions and disavowals. He could not bear to
think of her disillusionment. He felt that he owed
it to her not to disillusion her, to spoil things for
her in that fashion. "To turn into something
mean and ugly after she has believed in me. . . .
It would be like playing a practical joke upon her.
It would be like taking her into my arms and suddenly making a grimace at her. . . . It would scar
her with a second humiliation. . . ."

Should he take her on to Bath or Exeter to-morrow and contrive by some sudden arrival of tele-

grams that he had to go from her suddenly? But a mere sudden parting would not end things between them now unless he went off abruptly without explanations or any arrangements for further communications. At the outset of this escapade there had been a tacit but evident assumption that it was to end when she joined her father at Falmouth. It was with an effect of discovery that Sir Richmond realized that now it could not end in that fashion, that with the whisper of love and the touching of lips, something had been started that would go on, that would develop. To break off now and go away without a word would leave a raw and torn end, would leave her perplexed and perhaps even more humiliated with an aching mystery to distress her. "Why did he go? Was it something I said?—something he found out or imagined?"

Parting had disappeared as a possible solution of this problem. She and he had got into each other's lives to stay: the real problem was the terms upon which they were to stay in each other's lives. Close association had brought them to the point of being, in the completest sense, lovers; that could not be; and the real problem was the transmutation of their relationship to some form compatible with his honour and her happiness. A word, an idea, from some recent reading floated into Sir Richmond's head. "Sublimate," he whispered. "We have to sublimate this affair.

We have to put this relationship upon a Higher
Plane.''

His mind stopped short at that.

Presently his voice sounded out of the depths of
his heart. "God! How I loathe the Higher
Plane! . . .

"God has put me into this Higher Plane business like some poor little kid who has to wear
irons on its legs.

"I *want* her. . . . Do you hear, Martin? I
want her.''

As if by a lightning flash he saw his car with
himself and Miss Grammont—Miss Seyffert had
probably fallen out—traversing Europe and Asia
in headlong flight. To a sunlit beach in the South
Seas. . . .

His thoughts presently resumed as though these
unmannerly and fantastic interruptions had not
occurred.

"We have to carry the whole affair on to a
Higher Plane—and keep it there. We two love
one another—that has to be admitted now. (I
ought never to have touched her. I ought never
to have thought of touching her.) But we two
are too high, our aims and work and obligations
are too high for any ordinary love making. That
sort of thing would embarrass us, would spoil
everything.

"Spoil everything," he repeated, rather like a
small boy who learns an unpalatable lesson.

For a time Sir Richmond, exhausted by moral effort, lay staring at the darkness.

"It has to be done. I believe I can carry her through with it if I can carry myself. She's a finer thing than I am. . . . On the whole I am glad it's only one more day. Belinda will be about. . . . Afterwards we can write to each other. . . . If we can get over the next day it will be all right. Then we can write about .fuel and politics—and there won't be her voice and her presence. We shall really *sublimate*. . . . First class idea,—sublimate! . . . And I will go back to dear old Martin who's all alone there and miserable; I'll be kind to her and play my part and tell her her Carbuncle scar rather becomes her. . . . And in a little while I shall be altogether in love with her again. . . .

"Queer what a brute I've always been to Martin."

"Queer that Martin can come in a dream to me and take the upper hand with me. . . .

"Queer that *now*—I love Martin."

He thought still more profoundly. "By the time the Committee meets again I shall have been tremendously refreshed."

He repeated:—"Put things on the Higher Plane and keep them there. Then go back to Martin. And so to the work. That's it. . . ."

Nothing so pacifies the mind as a clear-cut purpose. Sir Richmond fell asleep during the fourth recapitulation of this programme.

§ 3

When Miss Grammont appeared at breakfast Sir Richmond saw at once that she too had had a restless night. When she came into the little long breakfast room of the inn with its brown screens and its neat white tables it seemed to him that the Miss Grammont of his nocturnal speculations, the beautiful young lady who had to be protected and managed and loved unselfishly, vanished like some exorcised intruder. Instead was this real dear young woman, who had been completely forgotten during the reign of her simulacrum and who now returned completely remembered, familiar, friendly, intimate. She touched his hand for a moment, she met his eyes with the shadow of a smile in her own.

"Oranges!" said Belinda from the table by the window. "Beautiful oranges."

She had been preparing them, poor Trans-atlantic exile, after the fashion in which grape fruits are prepared upon liners and in the civilized world of the west. "He's getting us tea spoons," said Belinda, as they sat down.

"This is realler England than ever," she said. "I've been up an hour. I found a little path down to the river bank. It's the greenest morning world and full of wild flowers. Look at these."

"That's lady's smock," said Sir Richmond.
"It's not really a flower; it's a quotation from
Shakespear."

"And there are cowslips!"

"*Cuckoo buds of yellow hue. Do paint the
meadows with delight.* All the English flowers
come out of Shakespear. I don't know what we
did before his time."

The waiter arrived with the tea spoons for the
oranges.

Belinda, having distributed these, resumed her
discourse of enthusiasm for England. She asked
a score of questions about Gloucester and Chepstow, the Severn and the Romans and the Welsh,
and did not wait for the answers. She did not
want answers; she talked to keep things going.
Her talk masked a certain constraint that came
upon her companions after the first morning's
greetings were over.

Sir Richmond as he had planned upstairs produced two Michelin maps. "To-day," he said,
"we will run back to Bath—from which it will be
easy for you to train to Falmouth. We will go
by Monmouth and then turn back through the
Forest of Dean, where you will get glimpses of
primitive coal mines still worked by two men and
a boy with a windlass and a pail. Perhaps we will
go through Cirencester. I don't know. Perhaps
it is better to go straight to Bath. In the very
heart of Bath you will find yourselves in just the

same world you visited at Pompeii. Bath is
Pompeii overlaid by Jane Austen's England.''

He paused for a moment. ''We can wire to
your agents from here before we start and we can
pick up their reply at Gloucester or Nailsworth
or even Bath itself. So that if your father is
nearer than we suppose—— But I think to-morrow afternoon will be soon enough for Falmouth,
anyhow.''

He stopped interrogatively.

Miss Grammont's face was white. ''That will
do very well,'' she said.

§ 4

They started, but presently they came to high
banks that showed such masses of bluebells,
ragged Robin, great stitchwort and the like that
Belinda was not to be restrained. She clamoured
to stop the car and go up the bank and pick her
hands full, and so they drew up by the roadside
and Sir Richmond and Miss Grammont sat down
near the car while Belinda carried her enthusiastic
onslaught on the flowers up the steep bank and
presently out of earshot.

The two lovers said unheeded things about the
flowers to each other and then fell silent. Then
Miss Grammont turned her head and seemed deliberately to measure her companion's distance.
Evidently she judged her out of earshot.

"Well," said Miss Grammont in her soft even voice. "We love one another. Is that so still?"

"I could not love you more."

"It wasn't a dream?"

"No."

"And to-morrow we part?"

He looked her in the eyes. "I have been thinking of that all night," he said at last.

"I too."

"And you think——?"

"That we must part. Just as we arranged it—when was it? Three days or three ages ago? There is nothing else in the world to do except for us to go our ways. . . . I love you. That means for a woman—— It means that I want to be with you. But that is impossible. . . . Don't doubt whether I love you because I say—impossible. . . ."

Sir Richmond, faced with his own nocturnal decision, was now moved to oppose it flatly. "Nothing that one can do is impossible."

She glanced again at Belinda and bent down towards him. "Suppose," she said, "you got back into that car with me; suppose that instead of going on as we have planned, you took me—away. How much of us would go?"

"You would go," said Sir Richmond, "and my heart."

"And this work of yours? And your honour? For the honour of a man in this New Age of

yours will be first of all in the work he does for the
world. And you will leave your work—to be just
a lover. And the work that I might do—because
of my father's wealth; all that would vanish too.
We should leave all of that, all of our usefulness,
all that much of ourselves. But what has made
me love you? Just your breadth of vision, just
the sense that you mattered. What has made you
love me? Just that I have understood the dream
of your work. All that we should have to leave
behind. We should specialize, in our own scandal.
We should run away just for one thing. To think,
by sharing the oldest, simplest, dearest indul-
gences in the world, that we had got each other.
When really we had lost each other, lost all that
mattered. . . .''

Her face was flushed with the earnestness of her
conviction. Her eyes were bright with tears.
''Don't think I don't love you. It's so hard to say
all this. Somehow it seems like going back on
something—something supreme. Our instincts
have got us. . . . Don't think I'd hold myself
from you, dear. I'd give myself to you with both
hands. I love you—— When a woman loves—I
at any rate—she loves altogether. But this thing
—I am convinced—cannot be. I must go,my own
way, the way I have to go. My father is the
strangest man, obstinate, more than half a savage.
For me—I know it—he has the jealousy of ten
husbands. If you take me—— If our secret be-

comes manifest—— If you are to take me and keep me, then his life and your life will become wholly this Feud, nothing but this Feud. You have to fight him anyhow—that is why I of all people must keep out of the quarrel. For him, it would be an immense excitement, full of the possibility of fierce satisfactions; for you, whether you won me or lost me, it would be utter waste and ruin.''

She paused and then went on:— ''And for me too, waste and ruin. I shall be a woman fought over. I shall be fought over as dogs fight over a bone. I shall sink back to the level of Helen of Troy. I shall cease to be a free citizen, a responsible free person. Whether you win me or lose me it will be waste and ruin for us both. Your Fuel Commission will go to pieces, all the wide, enduring work you have set me dreaming about will go the same way. We shall just be another romantic story. . . . No!''

Sir Richmond sat still, a little like a sullen child, she thought. ''I hate all this,'' he said slowly. ''I didn't think of your father before, and now I think of him it sets me bristling for a fight. It makes all this harder to give up. And yet, do you know, in the night I was thinking, I was coming to conclusions, very like yours. For quite other reasons. I thought we ought not to—— We have to keep friends anyhow and hear of each other?''

''That goes without saying.''

"I thought we ought not to go on to be lovers in any way that would affect you, touch you too closely. . . . I was sorry—I had kissed you."

"Not I. No. Don't be sorry for that. I am glad we have fallen in love, more glad than I have been of anything else in my life, and glad we have spoken plainly. . . . Though we have to part. . . . And——"

Her whisper came close to him. "For a whole day yet, all round the clock twice, you and I have one another."

Miss Seyffert began speaking as soon as she was well within earshot.

"I don't know the name of a single one of these flowers," she cried, "except the bluebells. Look at this great handful I've gotten! Springtime in Italy doesn't compare with it, not for a moment."

§ 5

Because Belinda Seyffert was in the dicky behind them with her alert interest in their emotions all too thinly and obviously veiled, it seemed more convenient to Sir Richmond and Miss Grammont to talk not of themselves but of Man and Woman and of that New Age according to the prophet Martineau, which Sir Richmond had partly described and mainly invented and ascribed to his departed friend. They talked anthropologically, philosophically, speculatively, with an absurd pretence of detachment, they sat side by side in the little car, scarcely glancing at one another, but side by side and touching each other, and all the while they were filled with tenderness and love and hunger for one another.

In the course of a day or so they had touched on nearly every phase in the growth of Man and Woman from that remote and brutish past which has left its traces in human bones mingled with the bones of hyænas and cave bears beneath the stalagmites of Wookey Hole near Wells. In those nearly forgotten days the mind of man and woman had been no more than an evanescent succession of monstrous and infantile imaginations. That brief journey in the west country had lit up phase after phase in the long teaching and discipline of man as he had developed depth of memory and fixity of purpose out of these raw beginnings, through the dreaming childhood of Avebury and Stonehenge and the crude boyhood of ancient wars and massacres. Sir Richmond recalled those phases now, and how, as they had followed one another, man's idea of woman and woman's idea of man had changed with them, until nowadays in the minds of civilized men brute desire and possession and a limitless jealousy had become almost completely overlaid by the desire for fellowship and a free mutual loyalty. "Overlaid," he said. "The older passions are still there

like the fires in an engine.'' He invented a saying
for Dr. Martineau that the Man in us to-day was
still the old man of Palæolithic times, with his
will, his wrath against the universe increased
rather than diminished. If to-day he ceases to
crack his brother's bones and rape and bully his
womenkind, it is because he has grown up to a
greater game and means to crack this world and
feed upon its marrow and wrench their secrets
from the stars.

And furthermore it would seem that the prophet
Martineau had declared that in this New Age that
was presently to dawn for mankind, jealousy was
to be disciplined even as we had disciplined lust
and anger; instead of ruling our law it was to be
ruled by law and custom. No longer were the
jealousy of strange peoples, the jealousy of ownership and the jealousy of sex to determine the
framework of human life. There was to be one
peace and law throughout the world, one economic
scheme and a universal freedom for men and
women to possess and give themselves.

''And how many generations yet must there be
before we reach that Utopia?'' Miss Grammont
asked.

''I wouldn't put it at a very great distance.''

''But think of all the confusions of the world!''

''Confusions merely. The world is just a muddle of states and religions and theories and stu-
pidities. There are great lumps of disorderly

strength in it, but as a whole it is a weak world. It goes on by habit. There's no great idea in possession and the only possible great idea is this one. The New Age may be nearer than we dare to suppose."

"If I could believe that!"

"There are many more people think as we do than you suppose. Are you and I such very strange and wonderful and exceptional people?"

"No. I don't think so."

"And yet the New World is already completely established in our hearts. What has been done in our minds can be done in most minds. In a little while the muddled angry mind of Man upon his Planet will grow clear and it will be this idea that will have made it clear. And then life will be very different for everyone. That tyranny of disorder which oppresses every life on earth now will be lifted. There will be less and less insecurity, less and less irrational injustice. It will be a better instructed and a better behaved world. We shall live at our ease, not perpetually anxious, not resentful and angry. And that will alter all the rules of love. Then we shall think more of the loveliness of other people because it will no longer be necessary to think so much of the dangers and weaknesses and pitifulnesses of other people. We shall not have to think of those who depend upon us for happiness and self-respect. We shall not have to choose between a wasteful fight for a personal end or the surrender of our heart's desire.''

''Heart's desire,'' she whispered. ''Am I indeed your heart's desire?''

Sir Richmond sank his head and voice in response.

''You are the best of all things. And I have to let you go.''

Sir Richmond suddenly remembered Miss Seyffert and half turned his face towards her. Her forehead was just visible over the hood of the open coupé. She appeared to be intelligently intent upon the scenery. Then he broke out suddenly into a tirade against the world. ''But I am bored by this jostling unreasonable world. At the bottom of my heart I am bitterly resentful to-day. This is a world of fools and brutes in which we live, a world of idiotic traditions, imbecile limitations, cowardice, habit, greed and mean cruelty. It is a slum of a world, a congested district, an insanitary jumble of souls and bodies. Every good thing, every sweet desire is thwarted—every one. I have to lead the life of a slum missionary, a sanitary inspector, an underpaid teacher. I am bored. Oh God! how I am bored! I am bored by our laws and customs. I am bored by our rotten empire and its empty monarchy. I am bored by its parades and its flags and its sham enthusiasms. I am bored by London and its life, by its smart life and by its servile life alike. I am bored by theatres and by books and by every sort of thing that people call pleasure. I am bored by the brag of people and the claims of people and the feelings of people. Damn people! I am bored by profiteers and by the snatching they call business enterprise. Damn every business man! I am bored by politics and the universal mismanagement of everything. I am bored by France, by Anglo-Saxondom, by German self-pity, by Bolshevik fanaticism. I am bored by these fools' squabbles that devastate the world. I am bored by Ireland, Orange and Green. Curse the Irish—north and south together! Lord! how I *hate* the Irish from Carson to the last Sinn Feiner! And I am bored by India and by Egypt. I am bored by Poland and by Islam. I am bored by anyone who professes to have rights. Damn their rights! Curse their rights! I am bored to death by this year and by last year and by the prospect of next year. I am bored—I am horribly bored—by my work. I am bored by every sort of renunciation. I want to live with the woman I love and I want to work within the limits of my capacity. Curse all—— Hullo! Damn his eyes!—Steady, ah! The spark! . . . Good! No skid.''

He had come round a corner at five and twenty miles an hour and had stopped his spark and pulled up neatly within a yard of the fore-wheel of a waggon that was turning in the road so as to block the way completely.

"That almost had me. . . ."

"And now you feel better?" said Miss Grammont.

"Ever so much," said Sir Richmond and chuckled.

The waggoner cleared the road and the car started up again.

For a minute or so neither spoke.

"You ought to be smacked hard for that outbreak,—my dear," said Miss Grammont.

"I ought—*my* dear. I have no right to be ill-tempered. We two are among the supremely fortunate ones of our time. We have no excuse for misbehaviour. Got nothing to grumble at. Always I am lucky. *That*—with the waggon—was a very near thing. God spoils us.

"We two," he went on, after a pause, "are among the most fortunate people alive. We are both rich and easily rich. That gives us freedoms few people have. We have a vision of the whole world in which we live. It's in a mess—but that is by the way. The mass of mankind never gets enough education to have even a glimpse of the world as a whole. They never get a chance to get the hang of it. It is really possible for us to do things that will matter in the world. All our time is our own; all our abilities we are free to use. Most people, most intelligent and educated people, are caught in cages of pecuniary necessity; they are tied to tasks they can't leave, they are driven and compelled and limited by circumstances they can never master. But we, if we have tasks, have tasks of our own choosing. We may not like the world, but anyhow we are free to do our best to alter it. If I were a clerk in Hoxton and you were a city typist, then we *might* swear.''

''It was you who swore,'' smiled Miss Grammont.

''It's the thought of that clerk in Hoxton and that city typist who really keep me at my work. Any smacking ought to come from them. I couldn't do less than I do in the face of their help-lessness. Nevertheless a day will come—through what we do and what we refrain from doing—when there will be no bound and limited clerks in Hoxton and no captive typists in the city. And nobody at all to consider.''

''According to the prophet Martineau,'' said Miss Grammont.

''And then you and I must contrive to be born again.''

''Heighho!'' cried Miss Grammont. ''A thou-sand years ahead! When fathers are civilized. When all these phanton people who intervene on your side—no! I don't want to know anything about them, but I know of them by instinct—when they also don't matter.''

''Then you and I can have things out with each other—*thoroughly,*'' said Sir Richmond, with a

surprising ferocity in his voice, charging the little
hill before him as though he charged at Time.

§ 6

They had to wait at Nailsworth for a telegram
from Mr. Grammont's agents; they lunched there
and drove on to Bath in the afternoon. They
came into the town through unattractive and un-
worthy outskirts, and only realized the charm of
the place after they had garaged their car at the
Pulteney Hotel and walked back over the Pulteney
Bridge to see the Avon and the Pump Room and
the Roman Baths. The *Pulteney* they found hung
with pictures and adorned with sculpture to an
astonishing extent; some former proprietor must
have had a mania for replicas and the place is
eventful with white marble fauns and sylphs and
lions and Cæsars and Queen Victorias and packed
like an exhibition with memories of Rome, Florence, Milan, Paris, the National Gallery and the
Royal Academy, amidst which splendours a competent staff administers modern comforts with
an old-fashioned civility. But round and about
the *Pulteney* one has still the scenery of Georgian
England, the white, faintly classical terraces and
houses of the days of Fielding, Smollett, Fanny
Burney and Jane Austen, the graceful bridge with
the bright little shops full of "presents from

Bath''; the Pump Room with its water drinkers and a fine array of the original Bath chairs.

Down below the Pump Room our travellers explored the memories of the days when the world was Latin from York to the Tigris, and the Corinthian capital flourished like a weed from Bath to Baalbek. And they considered a little doubtfully the seventeenth century statue of Bladud, who is said to have been healed by the Bath waters and to have founded the city in the days when Stonehenge still flourished, eight hundred years before the Romans came.

In the afternoon Miss Seyffert came with Sir Richmond and Miss Grammont and was very enthusiastic about everything, but in the evening after dinner it was clear that her rôle was to remain in the hotel. Sir Richmond and Miss Grammont went out into the moonlit gloaming; they crossed the bridge again and followed the road beside the river towards the old Abbey Church, that Lantern of the West. Away in some sunken gardens ahead of them a band was playing, and a cluster of little lights about the bandstand showed a crowd of people down below dancing on the grass. These little lights, these bobbing black heads and the lilting music, this little inflamed centre of throbbing sounds and ruddy illumination, made the dome of the moonlit world about it seem very vast and cool and silent. Our visitors began to realize that Bath could be very beautiful.

They went to the parapet above the river and stood there, leaning over it elbow to elbow and smoking cigarettes. Miss Grammont was moved to declare the Pulteney Bridge, with its noble arch, its effect of height over the swirling river, and the cluster of houses above, more beautiful than the Ponte Vecchio at Florence. Down below was a man in waders with a fishing-rod going to and fro along the foaming weir, and a couple of boys paddled a boat against the rush of the water lower down the stream.

"Dear England!" said Miss Grammont, surveying this gracious spectacle. "How full it is of homely and lovely and kindly things!"

"It is the home we come from."

"You belong to it still."

"No more than you do. I belong to a big overworking modern place called London which stretches its tentacles all over the world. I am as much a home-coming tourist as you are. Most of this western country I am seeing for the first time."

She said nothing for a space. "I've not a word to say to-night," she said. "I'm just full of a sort of animal satisfaction in being close to you. . . . And in being with you among lovely things. . . . Somewhere—— Before we part to-night—— . . ."

"Yes?" he said to her pause, and his face came very near to hers.

"I want you to kiss me."

"Yes," he said awkwardly, glancing over his shoulder, acutely aware of the promenaders passing close to them.

"It's a promise?"

"Yes."

Very timidly and guiltily his hand sought hers beside it and gripped it and pressed it. "My dear!" he whispered, tritest and most unavoidable of expressions. It was not very like Man and Woman loving upon their Planet; it was much more like the shy endearments of the shop boys and work girls who made the darkling populous about them with their silent interchanges.

"There are a thousand things I want to talk about to you," she said. "After we have parted to-morrow I shall begin to think of them. But now —every rational thing seems dissolved in this moonlight.". . .

Presently she made an effort to restore the intellectual dignity of their relationship.

"I suppose I ought to be more concerned to-night about the work I have to do in the world and anxious for you to tell me this and that, but indeed I am not concerned at all about it. I seem to have it in outline all perfectly clear. I mean to play a man's part in the world just as my father wants me to do. I mean to win his confidence and work with him—like a partner. Then some day I shall be a power in the world of fuel. And at the same time I must watch and read and think and learn how to be the servant of the world. . . . We two have to live like trusted servants who have been made guardians of a helpless minor. We have to put things in order and keep them in order against the time when Man—Man whom we call in America the Common Man—can take hold of his world——"

"And release his servants," said Sir Richmond.

"All that is perfectly clear in my mind. That is what I am going to live for; that is what I have to do."

She stopped abruptly. "All that is about as interesting to-night—in comparison with the touch of your dear fingers—as next month's railway time-table."

But later she found a topic that could hold their attention for a time.

"We have never said a word about religion," she said.

Sir Richmond paused for a moment. "I am a godless man," he said. "The stars and space and time overwhelm my imagination. I cannot imagine anything above or beyond them."

She thought that over. "But there are divine things," she said.

"*You* are divine. . . . I'm not talking lovers' nonsense," he hastened to add. "I mean that there is something about human beings—not just the everyday stuff of them, but something that appears intermittently—as though a light shone through something translucent. If I believe in any divinity at all it is a divinity revealed to me by other people—— And even by myself in my own heart.

"I'm never surprised at the badness of human beings," said Sir Richmond; "seeing how they have come about and what they are; but I have been surprised time after time by fine things. . . . Often in people I disliked or thought little of. . . . I can understand that I find you full of divine quality, because I am in love with you and all alive to you. Necessarily I keep on discovering loveliness in you. But I have seen divine things— in dear old Martineau, for example. A vain man, fussy, timid—and yet filled with a passion for truth, ready to make great sacrifices and to toil tremendously for that. And in those men I am always cursing, my Committee, it is astonishing at times to discover what streaks of goodness even the really bad men can show. . . . But one can't make use of just anyone's divinity. I can see the divinity in Martineau but it leaves me cold. He tired me and bored me. . . . But I live on you. It's only through love that the God can reach over from one human being to another. All real love is a divine thing, a reassurance, a release of courage. It is wonderful enough that we should take food and drink and turn them into imagination, invention and creative energy; it is still more wonderful that we should take an animal urging and turn it into a light to discover beauty and an impulse towards the utmost achievements of which we are capable. All love is a sacrament and all lovers are priests to each other. You and I——''

Sir Richmond broke off abruptly. "I spent three days trying to tell this to Dr. Martineau. But he wasn't the priest I had to confess to and the words wouldn't come. I can confess it to you readily enough. . . .''

"I cannot tell," said Miss Grammont, "whether this is the last wisdom in life or—moonshine. I cannot tell whether I am thinking or feeling; but the noise of the water going over the weir below is like the stir in my heart. And I am swimming in love and happiness. Am I awake or am I dreaming you, and are we dreaming one another? Hold my hand—hold it hard and tight. I'm trembling with love for you and all the world. . . . If I say more I shall be weeping.''

For a long time they stood side by side saying not a word to one another.

Presently the band down below and the dancing ceased and the little lights were extinguished. The silent moon seemed to grow brighter and larger and the whisper of the waters louder. A crowd of young people flowed out of the gardens and passed by on their way home. Sir Richmond and Miss Grammont strolled through the dispersing crowd and over the Toll Bridge and went exploring down a little staircase that went down from the end of the bridge to the dark river, and then came back to their old position at the parapet looking upon the weir and the Pulteney Bridge. The gardens that had been so gay were already dark and silent as they returned, and the streets echoed emptily to the few people who were still abroad.

"It's the most beautiful bridge in the world," said Miss Grammont, and gave him her hand again.

Some deep-toned clock close by proclaimed the hour eleven.

The silence healed again.

"Well?" said Sir Richmond.

"Well?" said Miss Grammont smiling very faintly.

"I suppose we must go out of all this beauty now, back to the lights of the hotel and the watchful eyes of your dragon."

"She has not been a very exacting dragon so far, has she?"

"She is a miracle of tact."

"She does not really watch. But she is curious —and very sympathetic."

"She is wonderful." . . .

"That man is still fishing," said Miss Grammont.

For a time she peered down at the dark figure wading in the foam below as though it was the

only thing of interest in the world. Then she
turned to Sir Richmond.

"I would trust Belinda with my life," she said.
"And anyhow—now—we need not worry about
Belinda."

§ 7

At the breakfast table it was Belinda who was
the most nervous of the three, the most moved,
the most disposed to throw a sacramental air over
their last meal together. Her companions had
passed beyond the idea of separation; it was as
if they now cherished a secret satisfaction at the
high dignity of their parting. Belinda in some
way perceived they had become different. They
were no longer tremulous lovers; they seemed sure
of one another and with a new pride in their bearing. It would have pleased Belinda better, seeing
how soon they were to be torn apart, if they had
not made quite such excellent breakfasts. She
even suspected them of having slept—well. Yet
yesterday they had been deeply stirred. They
had stayed out late last night, so late that she had
not heard them come in. Perhaps then they had
passed the climax of their emotions. Sir Richmond, she learnt, was to take the party to Exeter,
where there would be a train for Falmouth a little
after two. If they started from Bath about nine
that would give them an ample margin of time

in which to deal with a puncture or any such misadventure.

They crested the Mendips above Shepton Mallet, ran through Ilchester and Ilminster into the lovely hill country about Up-Ottery and so to Honiton and the broad level road to Exeter. Sir Richmond and Miss Grammont were in a state of happy gravity; they sat contentedly side by side, talking very little. They had already made their arrangements for writing to one another. There was to be no stream of love-letters or protestations. That might prove a mutual torment. Their love was to be implicit. They were to write at intervals about political matters and their common interests, and to keep each other informed of their movements about the world.

"We shall be working together," she said, speaking suddenly out of a train of thought she had been following, "we shall be closer together than many a couple who have never spent a day apart for twenty years."

Then presently she said: "In the New Age all lovers will have to be accustomed to meeting and parting. We women will not be tied very much by domestic needs. Unless we see fit to have children. We shall be going about our business like men; we shall have world-wide businesses—many of us—just as men will. . . .

"It will be a world full of lovers' meetings.

Some day—somewhere—we two will certainly
meet again.''

''Even you have to force circumstances a little,'' said Sir Richmond.

''We shall meet,'' she said, ''without doing
that.''

''But where?'' he asked unanswered. . . .

''Meetings and partings,'' she said. ''Women
will be used to seeing their lovers go away. Even
to seeing them go away to other women who have
borne them children and who have a closer claim
on them.''

''No one——'' began Sir Richmond, startled.

''But I don't mind very much. It's how things
are. If I were a perfectly civilized woman I
shouldn't mind at all. If men and women are not
to be tied to each other there must needs be such
things as this.''

''But you,'' said Sir Richmond. ''I at any rate
am not like that. I cannot bear the thought that
you——''

''You need not bear it, my dear. I was just
trying to imagine this world that is to be. Women
I think are different from men—in their jealousy.
Men are jealous of the other man; women are jealous for their man—and careless about the other
woman. What I love in you I am sure about. My
mind was empty when it came to you and now it is
full to overflowing. I shall feel you moving about

in the same world with me. I'm not likely to think
of anyone else for a very long time. . . . Later on,
who knows? I may marry. I make no vows. But
I think until I know certainly that you do not
want me any more it will be impossible for me to
marry or to have a lover. I don't know, but
that is how I believe it will be with me. And my
mind feels beautifully clear now and settled. I've
got your idea and made it my own, your idea that
we matter scarcely at all, but that the work we do
matters supremely. I'll find my rope and tug it,
never fear. Half way round the world perhaps
some day you will feel me tugging."

"I shall feel you're there," he said, "whether
you tug or not. . . .

"Three miles left to Exeter," he reported
presently.

She glanced back at Belinda.

"It is good that we have loved, my dear," she
whispered. "Say it is good."

"The best thing in all my life," he said, and
lowered his head and voice to say: "My dearest
dear."

"Heart's desire—still?"

"Heart's delight. . . . Priestess of life. . . .
Divinity."

She smiled and nodded and suddenly Belinda,
up above their lowered heads, accidentally and
irrelevantly, no doubt, coughed.

At Exeter Station there was not very much time

to spare after all. Hardly had Sir Richmond secured a luncheon basket for the two travellers before the train came into the station. He parted from Miss Grammont with a hand clasp. Belinda was flushed and distressed at the last but her friend was quiet and still. "Au revoir," said Belinda without conviction when Sir Richmond shook her hand.

§ 8.

Sir Richmond stood quite still on the platform as the train ran out of the station. He did not move until it had disappeared round the bend. Then he turned, lost in a brown study, and walked very slowly towards the station exit.

"The most wonderful thing in my life," he thought. "And already—it is unreal.

"She will go on to her father—whom she knows ten thousand times more thoroughly than she knows me; she will go on to Paris, she will pick up all the threads of her old story, be reminded of endless things in her life, but never except in the most casual way of these days: they will be cut off from everything else that will serve to keep them real; and as for me—this connects with nothing else in my life at all. . . . It is as disconnected as a dream. . . . Already it is hardly more substantial than a dream. . . .

"We shall write letters. Do letters breathe faster or slower as you read them?

"We may meet.

"Where are we likely to meet again? . . . I never realized before how improbable it is that we shall meet again. And if we meet? . . .

"Never in all our lives shall we be really *together* again. It's over—— With a completeness. . . .

"Like death."

He came opposite the bookstalls and stopped short and stared with unseeing eyes at the display of popular literature. He was wondering now whether after all he ought to have let her go. He experienced something of the blank amazement of a child who has burst its toy balloon. His golden globe of satisfaction in an instant had gone. An irrational sense of loss was flooding every other feeling about V.V. If she had loved him truly and altogether could she have left him like this? Neither of them surely had intended so complete a separation. He wanted to go back and recall that train.

A few seconds more, he realized, and he would give way to anger. Whatever happened that must not happen. He pulled himself together. What was it he had to do now? He had not to be angry, he had not even to be sorry. They had done the right thing. Outside the station his car was waiting.

He went outside the station and stared at his car. He had to go somewhere. Of course! down

into Cornwall to Martin's cottage. He had to go
down to her and be kind and comforting about that
carbuncle. To be kind? . . . If this thwarted
feeling broke out into anger he might be tempted
to take it out of Martin. That at any rate he must
not do. He had always for some inexplicable
cause treated Martin badly. Nagged her and
blamed her and threatened her. That must stop
now. No shadow of this affair must lie on Martin.
. . . And Martin must never have a suspicion of
any of this. . . .

The image of Martin became very vivid in his
mind. He thought of her as he had seen her many
times, with the tears close, fighting with her back
to the wall, with all her wit and vigour gone, because she loved him more steadfastly than he did
her. Whatever happened he must not take it out
of Martin. It was astonishing how real she had
become now—as V.V. became a dream. Yes,
Martin was astonishingly real. And if only he
could go now and talk to Martin—and face all the
facts of life with her, even as he had done with
that phantom Martin in his dream. . . .

But things were not like that.

He looked to see if his car was short of water
or petrol; both needed replenishing, and so he
would have to go up the hill into Exeter town
again. He got into his car and sat with his fingers on the electric starter.

Martin! Old Friend! Eight days were still left

before the Committee met again, eight days for golden kindness. He would distress Martin by no clumsy confession. He would just make her happy as she loved to be made happy. . . . Nevertheless. Nevertheless. . . .

Was it Martin who failed him or he who failed Martin?

Incessant and insoluble dispute. Well, the thing now was to go to Martin. . . . And then the work!

He laughed suddenly.

"I'll take it out of the damned Commission. I'll make old Rumford Brown sit up."

He was astonished to find himself thinking of the affairs of the Commission with a lively interest and no trace of fatigue. He had had his change; he had taken his rest; he was equal to his task again already. He started his engine and steered his way past a van and a waiting cab.

"Fuel," he said.

CHAPTER THE NINTH

THE LAST DAYS OF SIR RICHMOND HARDY

§ 1

THE Majority and Minority Reports of the Fuel
Commission were received on their first publication with much heat and disputation, but there is
already a fairly general agreement that they are
great and significant documents, broadly conceived and historically important. They do lift
the questions of fuel supply and distribution high
above the level of parochial jealousies and above
the petty and destructive profiteering of private
owners and traders, to a view of a general human
welfare. They form an important link in a series
of private and public documents that are slowly
opening out a prospect of new economic methods,
methods conceived in the generous spirit of scientific work, that may yet arrest the drift of our
western civilization towards financial and commer-
cial squalor and the social collapse that must ensue
inevitably on that. In view of the composition of
the Committee, the Majority Report is in itself an
amazing triumph of Sir Richmond's views; it is

astonishing that he was able to drive his opponents so far and then leave them there securely advanced while he carried on the adherents he had altogether won, including, of course, the labour representatives, to the further altitudes of the Minority Report.

After the summer recess the Majority Report was discussed and adopted. Sir Richmond had shown signs of flagging energy in June, but he had come back in September in a state of exceptional vigour; for a time he completely dominated the Committee by the passionate force of his convictions and the illuminating scorn he brought to bear on the various subterfuges and weakening amendments by which the meaner interests sought to save themselves in whole or in part from the common duty of sacrifice. But toward the end he fell ill. He had worked to the pitch of exhaustion. He neglected a cold that settled on his chest. He began to cough persistently and betray an increasingly irritable temper. In the last fights in the Committee his face was bright with fever and he spoke in a voiceless whisper, often a vast angry whisper. His place at table was marked with scattered lozenges and scraps of paper torn to the minutest shreds. Such good manners as had hitherto mitigated his behaviour on the Committee departed from him. He carried his last points, gesticulating and coughing and wheezing rather than speaking. But he had so hammered his ideas into the Committee that they took the effect of what he was trying to say.

He died of pneumonia at his own house three days after the passing of the Majority Report. The Minority Report, his own especial creation, he never signed. It was completed by Wast and Carmichael. . . .

After their parting at Salisbury station Dr. Martineau heard very little of Sir Richmond for a time except through the newspapers, which contained frequent allusions to the Committee. Someone told him that Sir Richmond had been staying at Ruan in Cornwall where Martin Leeds had a cottage, and someone else had met him at Bath on his way, he said, in his car from Cornwall to a conference with Sir Peter Davies in Glamorganshire.

But in the interim Dr. Martineau had the pleasure of meeting Lady Hardy at a luncheon party. He was seated next to her and he found her a very pleasing and sympathetic person indeed. She talked to him freely and simply of her husband and of the journey the two men had taken together. Either she knew nothing of the circumstances of their parting or if she did she did not betray her knowledge. "That holiday did him a world of good," she said. "He came back to his work like a giant. I feel very grateful to you."

Dr. Martineau said it was a pleasure to have helped Sir Richmond's work in any way. He believed in him thoroughly. Sir Richmond was inspired by great modern creative ideas.

"Forgive me if I keep you talking about him," said Lady Hardy. "I wish I could feel as sure that I had been of use to him."

Dr. Martineau insisted. "I know very well that you are."

"I do what I can to help him carry his enormous burthen of toil" she said. "I try to smooth his path. But he is a strange silent creature at times."

Her eyes scrutinized the doctor's face.

It was not the doctor's business to supplement Sir Richmond's silences. Yet he wished to meet the requirements of this lady if he could. "He is one of those men," he said, "who are driven by forces they do not fully understand. A man of genius."

"Yes," she said in an undertone of intimacy. "Genius. . . . A great irresponsible genius. . . . Difficult to help. . . . I wish I could do more for him."

A very sweet and charming lady. It was with great regret that the doctor found the time had come to turn to his left-hand neighbour.

§ 2

It was with some surprise that Dr. Martineau received a fresh appeal for aid from Sir Richmond. It was late in October and Sir Richmond was already seriously ill. But he was still going about his business as though he was perfectly well. He had not mistaken his man. Dr. Martineau received him as though there had never been a shadow of offence between them.

He came straight to the point. "Martineau," he said, "I must have those drugs I asked you for when first I came to you now. I must be bolstered up. I can't last out unless I am. I'm at the end of my energy. I come to you because you will understand. The Commission can't go on now for more than another three weeks. Whatever happens afterwards I must keep going until then."

The doctor did understand. He made no vain objections. He did what he could to patch up his friend for his last struggles with the opposition in the Committee. "Pro forma," he said, stethoscope in hand, "I must order you to bed. You won't go. But I order you. You must know that what you are doing is risking your life. Your lungs are congested, the bronchial tubes already. That may spread at any time. If this open weather lasts you may go about and still pull through. But at any time this may pass into pneumonia. And there's not much in you just now to stand up against pneumonia. . . . ."

"I'll take all reasonable care."

"Is your wife at home?"

"She is in Wales with her people. But the household is well trained. I can manage."

"Go in a closed car from door to door. Wrap up like a mummy. I wish the Committee room wasn't down those abominable House of Commons corridors. . . ."

They parted with an affectionate handshake.

§ 3

Death approved of Sir Richmond's determination to see the Committee through. Our universal creditor gave this particular debtor grace to the very last meeting. Then he brushed a gust of chilly rain across the face of Sir Richmond as he stood waiting for his car outside the strangers' entrance to the House. For a couple of days Sir Richmond felt almost intolerably tired, but scarcely noted the changed timbre of the wheezy notes in his throat. He rose later each day and with ebbing vigour, jotted down notes and corrections upon the proofs of the Minority Report. He found it increasingly difficult to make decisions; he would correct and alter back and then repeat the correction, perhaps half a dozen times. On the evening of the second day his lungs became painful and his breathing difficult. His head ached and a sense of some great impending evil came upon him. His skin was suddenly a detestable garment to wear. He took his temperature with a little clinical thermometer he kept by him and found it was a hundred and one. He telephoned hastily for Dr. Martineau and without waiting for his arrival, took a hot bath and got into bed. He was already thoroughly ill when the doctor arrived.

"Forgive my sending for you," he said. "Not your line. I know. . . . My wife's G.P.—an exasperating sort of ass. Can't stand him. No one else."

He was lying on a narrow little bed with a hard pillow that the doctor replaced by one from Lady Hardy's room. He had twisted the bed-clothes into a hopeless muddle, the sheet was on the floor.

Sir Richmond's bedroom was a large apartment in which sleep seemed to have been an admitted necessity rather than a principal purpose. On one hand it opened into a business-like dressing and bath room, on the other into the day study. It bore witness to the nocturnal habits of a man who had long lived a life of irregular impulses to activity and dislocated hours and habits. There was a desk and reading lamp for night work near the fireplace, an electric kettle for making tea at night, a silver biscuit tin; all the apparatus for the lonely intent industry of the small hours. There was a bookcase of bluebooks, books of reference and suchlike material, and some files. Over the mantelpiece was an enlarged photograph of Lady Hardy and a plain office calendar. The desk was littered with the galley proofs of the Minority Report upon which Sir Richmond had been working up to the moment of his hasty retreat to bed. And lying among the proofs, as though it had been taken out and looked at quite recently, was the photograph of a girl. For a moment Dr. Martineau's mind hung in doubt and then he knew it for the young American of Stonehenge. How that affair had ended he did not know. And now it was not his business to know.

These various observations printed themselves on Dr. Martineau's mind after his first cursory examination of his patient and while he cast about for anything that would give this large industrious apartment a little more of the restfulness and comfort of a sick room. "I must get in a night nurse at once," he said. "We must find a small table somewhere to put near the bed.

"I am afraid you are very ill," he said, returning to the bedside. "This is not, as you say, my sort of work. Will you let me call in another man, a man we can trust thoroughly, to consult?"

"I'm in your hands," said Sir Richmond. "I want to pull through."

"He will know better where to get the right sort of nurse for the case—and everything." . . .

The second doctor presently came, with the right sort of nurse hard on his heels. Sir Richmond submitted almost silently to his expert handling and was sounded and looked to and listened at.

"H'm," said the second doctor, and then encouragingly to Sir Richmond: "We've got to take care of you.

"There's a lot about this I don't like," said the second doctor and drew Dr. Martineau by the arm towards the study. For a moment or so Sir Richmond listened to the low murmur of their voices, but he did not feel very deeply interested in what they were saying. He began to think what a decent chap Dr. Martineau was, how helpful and fine and forgiving his professional training had made him, how completely he had ignored the smothered incivilities of their parting at Salisbury. All men ought to have some such training. Not a bad idea to put every boy and girl through a year or so of hospital service. . . . Sir Richmond must have dozed, for his next perception was of Dr. Martineau standing over him and saying, "I am afraid, my dear Hardy, that you are very ill indeed. Much more so than I thought you were at first."

Sir Richmond's raised eyebrows conveyed that he accepted this fact.

"I think Lady Hardy ought to be sent for."

Sir Richmond shook his head with unexpected vigour.

"Don't want her about," he said, and after a pause, "Don't want anybody about."

"But if anything happens——?"

"Send then."

An expression of obstinate calm overspread Sir

Richmond's face. He seemed to regard the matter as settled. He closed his eyes.

For a time Dr. Martineau desisted. He went to the window and turned to look again at the impassive figure on the bed. Did Sir Richmond fully understand? He made a step towards his patient and hesitated. Then he brought a chair and sat down at the bedside.

Sir Richmond opened his eyes and regarded him with a slight frown.

"A case of pneumonia," said the doctor, "after great exertion and fatigue, may take very rapid and unexpected turns."

Sir Richmond, cheek on pillow, seemed to assent.

"I think if you want to be sure that Lady Hardy sees you again—— . . . If you don't want to take risks about that—— . . . One never knows in these cases. Probably there is a night train."

Sir Richmond manifested no surprise at the warning. But he stuck to his point. His voice was faint but firm. "Couldn't make up anything to say to her. Anything she'd like."

Dr. Martineau rested on that for a little while. Then he said: "If there is anyone else?"

"Not possible," said Sir Richmond, with his eyes on the ceiling.

"But to see?"

Sir Richmond turned his head to Dr. Martineau. His face puckered like a peevish child's. "They'd want things said to them. . . . Things to remember. . . . I *can't*. I'm tired out."

"Don't trouble," whispered Dr. Martineau, suddenly remorseful.

But Sir Richmond also was remorseful. "Give them my love," he said. "Best love. . . . Old Martin. Love. . . ."

Dr. Martineau was turning away when Sir Richmond spoke again in a whisper. "Best love. . . . Poor at the best. . . ."

He dozed for a time. Then he made a great effort. "I can't see them, Martineau, until I've something to say. It's like that. Perhaps I shall think of some kind things to say—after a sleep. But if they came now. . . . I'd say something wrong. Be cross perhaps. Hurt someone. I've hurt so many. . . . People exaggerate. . . . People exaggerate—importance these occasions."

"Yes, yes," whispered Dr. Martineau. "I quite understand."

§ 4

For a time Sir Richmond dozed. Then he stirred and muttered. "Second rate. . . . Poor at the best. . . . Love. . . . Work. All. . . ."

"It has been splendid work," said Dr. Martineau, and was not sure that Sir Richmond heard.

"Those last few days . . . lost my grip. . . . Always lose my damned grip.

"Ragged them. . . . Put their backs up. . . . Silly. . . .

"Never. . . . Never done anything—*well*. . . .

"It's done. Done. Well or ill. . . .

"Done."

His voice sank to the faintest whisper. "Done for ever and ever . . . and ever . . . and ever."

Again he seemed to doze.

Dr. Martineau stood up softly. Something beyond reason told him that this was certainly a dying man. He was reluctant to go and he had an absurd desire that someone, someone for whom Sir Richmond cared, should come and say goodbye to him, and for Sir Richmond to say good-bye to someone. He hated this lonely launching from the shores of life of one who had sought intimacy so persistently and vainly. It was extraordinary —he saw it now for the first time—he loved this man. If it had been in his power, he would at that moment have anointed him with kindness.

The doctor found himself standing in front of the untidy writing desk, littered like a recent battlefield. The photograph of the American girl drew his eyes. What had happened? Was there not perhaps some word for her? He turned about as if to enquire of the dying man and found Sir Richmond's eyes open and regarding him. In them he saw an expression he had seen there once or twice before, a faint but excessively irritating gleam of amusement.

"Oh!—*Well!*" said Dr. Martineau and turned away. He went to the window and stared out as his habit was.

Sir Richmond continued to smile dimly at the doctor's back until his eyes closed again.

It was their last exchange. Sir Richmond died that night in the small hours, so quietly that for some time the night nurse did not observe what had happened. She was indeed roused to that realization by the ringing of the telephone bell in the adjacent study.

§ 5

For a long time that night Dr. Martineau had lain awake unable to sleep. He was haunted by the figure of Sir Richmond lying on his uncomfortable little bed in his big bedroom and by the curious effect of loneliness produced by the nocturnal desk and by the evident dread felt by Sir Richmond of any death-bed partings. He realized how much this man, who had once sought so feverishly for intimacies, had shrunken back upon himself, how solitary his motives had become, how rarely he had taken counsel with anyone in his later years. His mind now dwelt apart. Even if people came about him he would still be facing death alone.

And so it seemed he meant to slip out of life, as a man might slip out of a crowded assembly, unobserved. Even now he might be going. The doctor recalled how he and Sir Richmond had talked of the rage of life in a young baby, how we drove into life in a sort of fury, how that rage impelled us to do this and that, how we fought and struggled until the rage spent itself and was gone. That eddy of rage that was Sir Richmond was now perhaps very near its end. Presently it would fade and cease, and the stream that had made it and borne it would know it no more.

Dr. Martineau's thoughts relaxed and passed into the picture land of dreams. He saw the figure of Sir Richmond, going as it were away from him along a narrow path, a path that followed the crest of a ridge, between great darknesses, enormous cloudy darknesses, above him and below. He was going along this path without looking back, without a thought for those he left behind, without a single word to cheer him on his way, walking as Dr. Martineau had sometimes watched him walking, without haste or avidity, walking as a man might along some great picture gallery with which he was perhaps even over familiar. His hands would be in his pockets, his indifferent eyes upon the clouds about him. And as he strolled along that path, the darkness closed in upon him. His figure became dim and dimmer.

Whither did that figure go? Did that enveloping darkness hide the beginnings of some strange long journey or would it just dissolve that figure into itself?

Was that indeed the end?

Dr. Martineau was one of that large class of people who can neither imagine nor disbelieve in immortality. Dimmer and dimmer grew the figure but still it remained visible. As one can continue to see a star at dawn until one turns away. Or one blinks or nods and it is gone.

Vanished now are the beliefs that held our race for countless generations. Where now was that Path of the Dead, mapped so clearly, faced with such certainty, in which the heliolithic peoples believed from Avebury to Polynesia? Not always have we had to go alone and unprepared into uncharted darknesses. For a time the dream artist used a palette of the doctor's vague memories of things Egyptian, he painted a new roll of the Book of the Dead, at a copy of which the doctor had been looking a day or so before. Sir Richmond became a brown naked figure, crossing a bridge of danger, passing between terrific monsters, ferrying a dark and dreadful stream. He came to the scales of judgment before the very throne of Osiris and stood waiting while dog-headed Anubis weighed his conscience and that evil monster, the Devourer of the Dead, crouched ready if the judgment went against him. The doctor's attention concentrated upon the scales. A memory of Swedenborg's *Heaven and Hell* mingled with the Egyptian fantasy. Now at last it was possible to know something real about this

man's soul, now at last one could look into the
Secret Places of his Heart. Anubis and Thoth,
the god with the ibis head, were reading the heart
as if it were a book, reading aloud from it to the
supreme judge.

Suddenly the doctor found himself in his own
dreams. His anxiety to plead for his friend had
brought him in. He too had become a little
painted figure and he was bearing a book in his
hand. He wanted to show that the laws of the
new world could not be the same as those of the
old, and the book he was bringing as evidence was
his own *Psychology of a New Age.*

The clear thought of that book broke up his
dream by releasing a train of waking troubles.
. . . You have been six months on Chapter Ten;
will it ever be ready for Osiris? . . . Will it
ever be ready for print? . . .

Dream and waking thoughts were mingled like
sky and cloud upon a windy day in April. Suddenly he saw again that lonely figure on the narrow way with darknesses above and darknesses
below and darknesses on every hand. But this
time it was not Sir Richmond. . . . Who was
it? Surely it was Everyman. Everyman had to
travel at last along that selfsame road, leaving
love, leaving every task and every desire. But was
it Everyman? . . . A great fear and horror came
upon the doctor. That little figure was himself!
And the book which was his particular task in

life was still undone. He himself stood in his
turn upon that lonely path with the engulfing
darknesses about him. . . .

He seemed to wrench himself awake.

He lay very still for some moments and then
he sat up in bed. An overwhelming conviction
had arisen in his mind that Sir Richmond was
dead. He felt he must know for certain. He
switched on his electric light, mutely interrogated
his round face reflected in the looking glass, got
out of bed, shuffled on his slippers and went
along the passage to the telephone. He hesitated
for some seconds and then lifted the receiver.
It was his call which aroused the nurse to the
fact of Sir Richmond's death.

§ 6

Lady Hardy arrived home in response to Dr.
Martineau's telegram late on the following evening. He was with her next morning, comforting
and sympathetic. Her big blue eyes, bright with
tears, met his very wistfully; her little body
seemed very small and pathetic in its simple black
dress. And yet there was a sort of bravery about
her. When he came into the drawing-room she
was in one of the window recesses talking to a
serious-looking woman of the dressmaker type.
She left her business at once to come to him.
"Why did I not know in time?" she cried.

"No one, dear lady, had any idea until late last night," he said, taking both her hands in his for a long friendly sympathetic pressure.

"I might have known that if it had been possible you would have told me," she said.

"You know," she added, "I don't believe it yet. I don't realize it. I go about these formalities——"

"I think I can understand that."

"He was always, you know, not quite here. . . . It is as if he were a little more not quite here. . . . I can't believe it is over. . . ."

She asked a number of questions and took the doctor's advice upon various details of the arrangements. "My daughter Helen comes home to-morrow afternoon," she explained. "She is in Paris. But our son is far, far away in the Punjab. I have sent him a telegram. . . . It is so kind of you to come in to me."

Dr. Martineau went more than half way to meet Lady Hardy's disposition to treat him as a friend of the family. He had conceived a curious, half maternal affection for Sir Richmond that had survived even the trying incident of the Salisbury parting and revived very rapidly during the last few weeks. This affection extended itself now to Lady Hardy. Hers was a type that had always appealed to him. He could understand so well the perplexed loyalty with which she was now setting herself to gather together some pre-

servative and reassuring evidences of this man
who had always been; as she put it, "never quite
here." It was as if she felt that now it was at
last possible to make a definite reality of him. He
could be fixed. And as he was fixed he would stay.
Never more would he be able to come in and with
an almost expressionless glance wither the inter-
pretation she had imposed upon him. She was
finding much comfort in this task of reconstruction. She had gathered together in the drawing-
room every presentable portrait she had been able
to find of him. He had never, she said, sat to a
painter, but there was an early pencil sketch done
within a couple of years of their marriage; there
was a number of photographs, several of which—
she wanted the doctor's advice upon this point—
she thought might be enlarged; there was a statuette done by some woman artist who had once
beguiled him into a sitting. There was also a
painting she had had worked up from a photograph and some notes. She flitted among these
memorials, going from one to the other, undecided
which to make the standard portrait. "That
painting, I think, is most like," she said: "as he
was before the war. But the war and the Commission changed him,—worried him and aged
him. . . . I grudged him to that Commission. He
let it worry him frightfully."

"It meant very much to him," said Dr. Martineau.

"It meant too much to him. But of course his ideas were splendid. You know it is one of my hopes to get some sort of book done, explaining his ideas. He would never write. He despised it—unreasonably. A real thing done, he said, was better than a thousand books. Nobody read books, he said, but women, parsons and idle people. But there must be books. And I want one. Something a little more real than the ordinary official biography. . . . I have thought of young Leighton, the secretary of the Commission. He seems thoroughly intelligent and sympathetic and really anxious to reconcile Richmond's views with those of the big business men on the Committee. He might do. . . . Or perhaps I might be able to persuade two or three people to write down their impressions of him. A sort of memorial volume. . . . But he was shy of friends. There was no man he talked to very intimately about his ideas unless it was to you . . . I wish I had the writer's gift, doctor."

§ 7

It was on the second afternoon that Lady Hardy summoned Dr. Martineau by telephone. "Something rather disagreeable," she said. "If you could spare the time. If you could come round.

"It is frightfully distressing," she said when he got round to her, and for a time she could tell him nothing more. She was having tea and she

gave him some. She fussed about with cream
and cakes and biscuits. He noted a crumpled
letter thrust under the edge of the silver tray.

"He talked, I know, very intimately with you,"
she said, coming to it at last. "He probably
went into things with you that he never talked
about with anyone else. Usually he was very reserved. Even with me there were things about
which he said nothing."

"We did," said Dr. Martineau with discretion,
"deal a little with his private life."

"There was someone——"

Dr. Martineau nodded and then, not to be too
portentous, took and bit a biscuit.

"Did he by any chance ever mention someone
called Martin Leeds?"

Dr. Martineau seemed to reflect. Then realiz-
ing that this was a mistake, he said: "He told
me the essential facts."

The poor lady breathed a sigh of relief. "I'm
glad," she said simply. She repeated, "Yes, I'm
glad. It makes things easier now."

Dr. Martineau looked his enquiry.

"She wants to come and see him."

"Here?"

"Here! And Helen here! And the servants
noticing everything! I've never met her. Never
set eyes on her. For all I know she may want to
make a scene." There was infinite dismay in her
voice.

Dr. Martineau was grave. "You would rather not receive her?"

"I don't want to refuse her. I don't want even to seem heartless. I understand, of course, she has a sort of claim." She sobbed her reluctant admission. "I know it. I know. . . . There was much between them."

Dr. Martineau pressed the limp hand upon the little tea table. "I understand, dear lady," he said. "I understand. Now . . . suppose *I* were to write to her and arrange—— I do not see that you need be put to the pain of meeting her. Suppose I were to meet her here myself?"

"If you *could!*"

The doctor was quite prepared to save the lady any further distresses, no matter at what trouble to himself. "You are so good to me," she said, letting the tears have their way with her.

"I am silly to cry," she said, dabbing her eyes.

"We will get it over to-morrow," he reassured her. "You need not think of it again."

He took over Martin's brief note to Lady Hardy and set to work by telegram to arrange for her visit. She was in London at her Chelsea flat and easily accessible. She was to come to the house at mid-day on the morrow, and to ask not for Lady Hardy but for him. He would stay by her while she was in the house, and it would be quite easy for Lady Hardy to keep herself and her daughter

out of the way. They could, for example, go out
quietly to the dressmakers in the closed car, for
many little things about the mourning still remained to be seen to.

§ 8

Miss Martin Leeds arrived punctually, but the
doctor was well ahead of his time and ready to
receive her. She was ushered into the drawing-
room where he awaited her. As she came forward the doctor first perceived that she had a
very sad and handsome face, the face of a sensitive youth rather than the face of a woman. She
had fine grey eyes under very fine brows; they
were eyes that at other times might have laughed
very agreeably, but which were now full of an
unrestrained sadness. Her brown hair was very
untidy and parted at the side like a man's. Then
he noted that she seemed to be very untidily
dressed as if she was that rare and, to him, very
offensive thing, a woman careless of her beauty.
She was short in proportion to her broad figure
and her broad forehead.

"You are Dr. Martineau?" she said. "He
talked of you." As she spoke her glance went
from him to the pictures that stood about the
room. She walked up to the painting and stood in
front of it with her distressed gaze wandering
about her. "Horrible!" she said. "Absolutely
horrible! . . . Did *she* do this?"

Her question disconcerted the doctor very much. "You mean Lady Hardy?" he asked. "She doesn't paint."

"No, no. I mean, did she get all these things together?"

"Naturally," said Dr. Martineau.

"None of them are a bit like him. They are like blows aimed at his memory. Not one has his life in it. How could she do it? Look at that idiot statuette! . . . He was extraordinarily difficult to get. I have burnt every photograph I had of him. For fear that this would happen; that he would go stiff and formal—just as you have got him here. I have been trying to sketch him almost all the time since he died. But I can't get him back. He's gone."

She turned to the doctor again. She spoke to him, not as if she expected him to understand her, but because she had to say these things which burthened her mind to someone. "I have done hundreds of sketches. My room is littered with them. When you turn them over he seems to be lurking among them. But not one of them is like him."

She was trying to express something beyond her power. "It is as if someone had suddenly turned out the light."

She followed the doctor upstairs. "This was his study," the doctor explained.

"I know it. I came here once," she said.

They entered the big bedroom in which the coffined body lay. Dr. Martineau, struck by a sudden memory, glanced nervously at the desk, but someone had made it quite tidy and the portrait of Miss Grammont had disappeared. Miss Leeds walked straight across to the coffin and stood looking down on the waxen inexpressive dignity of the dead. Sir Richmond's brows and nose had become sharper and more clear-cut than they had ever been in life and his lips had set into a faint inane smile. She stood quite still for a long time. At length she sighed deeply.

She spoke, a little as though she thought aloud, a little as though she talked at that silent presence in the coffin. "I think he loved," she said. "Sometimes I think he loved me. But it is hard to tell. He was kind. He could be intensely kind and yet he didn't seem to care for you. He could be intensely selfish and yet he certainly did not care for himself. . . . Anyhow, I loved *him*. . . . There is nothing left in me now to love anyone else—for ever. . . ."

She put her hands behind her back and looked at the dead man with her head a little on one side. "Too kind," she said very softly.

"There was a sort of dishonesty in his kindness. He would not let you have the bitter truth. He would not say he did not love you. . . .

"He was too kind to life ever to call it the foolish thing it is. He took it seriously because it takes itself seriously. He worked for it and killed himself with work for it. . . ."

She turned to Dr. Martineau and her face was streaming with tears. "And life, you know, isn't to be taken seriously. It is a joke—a bad joke—made by some cruel little god who has caught a neglected planet. . . . Like torturing a stray cat. . . . But he took it seriously and he gave up his life for it.

"There was much happiness he might have had. He was very capable of happiness. But he never seemed happy. This work of his came before it. He overworked and fretted our happiness away. He sacrificed his happiness and mine."

She held out her hands towards the doctor. "What am I to do now with the rest of my life? Who is there to laugh with me now and jest?

"I don't complain of him. I don't blame him. He did his best—to be kind.

"But all my days now I shall mourn for him and long for him. . . ."

She turned back to the coffin. Suddenly she lost every vestige of self-control. She sank down on her knees beside the trestle. "Why have you left me?" she cried.

"Oh! Speak to me, my darling! Speak to me, *I tell you!* Speak to me!"

It was a storm of passion, monstrously childish and dreadful. She beat her hands upon the coffin. She wept loudly and fiercely as a child does. . . .

Dr. Martineau drifted feebly to the window.

He wished he had locked the door. The servants might hear and wonder what it was all about. Always he had feared love for the cruel thing it was, but now it seemed to him for the first time that he realized its monstrous cruelty.

THE END